FIRE

WIGGOTT'S WONDERFUL WAXWORLD

FLIGHT

FIRE

WIGGOTT'S WONDERFUL WAXWORLD

FLIGHT

TERRY DEARY

SCHOLASTIC

Scholastic Children's Books
An imprint of Scholastic Ltd
Euston House, 24 Eversholt Street, London, NW1 1DB, UK
Registered office: Westfield Road, Southam, Warwickshire, CV47 0RA
SCHOLASTIC and associated logos are trademarks and/or
registered trademarks of Scholastic Inc.

First published in the UK by Scholastic Ltd, 2019

ISBN 978 1407 19684 8

A CIP catalogue record of this book
is available from the British Library.

Printed by CPI Group (UK) Ltd, Croydon, CR0 4YY
Papers used by Scholastic Children's Books are made
from wood grown in sustainable forests.

1 3 5 7 9 10 8 6 4 2

www.scholastic.co.uk

This book is written in tribute to
G.K. Chesterton (1874–1936) and his book
The Napoleon of Notting Hill

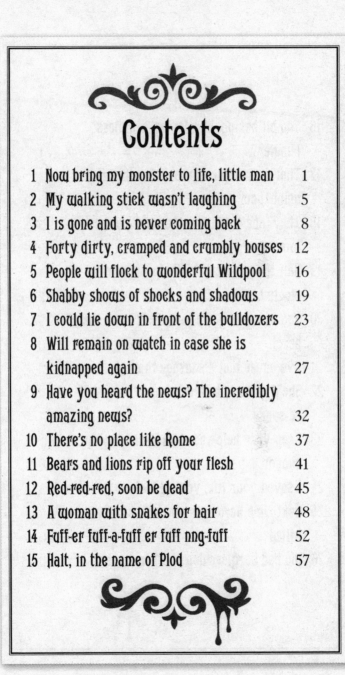

Contents

Now bring my monster to life, little man

The monster lay on a table. It was an ugly creature with stitches holding its body parts together and a bolt through the neck to keep its head from falling off.

A woman in a scarlet dress and rose-red high-heeled shoes looked down on the lifeless form. Even the soles of her shoes were red (though I can't see the point of that, myself). Her necklace and bracelets and rings were rich rubies. Her fingernails were reddest of all, red as fresh blood[1].

A man stood beside her. A small man who twitched and shivered with nerves. He wore a

---

1 I think you get the idea. Red was her favourite colour. Now let's get back to the monster, who wasn't even the palest shade of pink.

patch over one eye – some days it was the right eye and some days it was the left eye. He only wore it to make him look sinister, menacing, evil, creepy and baleful. He dressed in baleful black and wore baleful black boots. It was enough to scare a classful of infant children . . . but not you. Obviously.

'Are you ready to switch on the power, Igon?' the woman asked.

'My name is Igor,' the little man croaked.

'Your eye is gone, so you will always be I-gon to me,' she snapped, and her chins jiggled.

'Yes, Lady Greystone,' he sighed.

She squinted at him through her small and narrow eyes. 'Lady Greystone is wanted by the police, Igon. I have changed my name to Lady Frankenstone instead.'

'That'll fool them,' Igon muttered.

'Now bring my monster to life, little man.'

Igon gave a nervous cough. 'Strictly speaking, it is MY monster. I created the infinit-G microchip. The one that turns plastic gloop into flesh and changes lifeless matter into brains.'

'And it is MY money that bought this fine

building for you to work in. I pay all the white-coated evil assistants that every evil inventor needs. MY money that bought Loaf Tower for you to practise your dark arts ... and MY money that pays for the tea and sticky buns that the white-coat workers love so much.' She glared down at him. 'So, Igon, whose monster is this?'

'Yours,' he whispered.

'Louder, Igon.'

'Yours. Lady. Grey. Stone,' he screamed. Then said quietly, 'I mean, Lady Frankenstone.'

'So, press the switch.'

He pressed the button on a controller that looked like a smartphone. The monster began to breathe. A rasping, gasping breath. Its eyes fluttered open. Wide eyes, wild eyes, wondersome eyes. Its jaw wobbled, its mouth opened, and it gave a cheerful smile. It spoke. 'Ooooh, hell-oooo. It's nice to meet you. Ooooh, may I say what a pleasure it is to be here? And I really look forward to making new friends and having fun. Ooooh, hell-oooo.'

Lady Frankenstone's little eyes shrank to tiny purple raisins and she turned them on Igon.

'It is supposed to be a fearsome creature that will terrify visitors, not an entertainer for a child's fifth birthday party. Start again!'

Igon sighed and pressed a button. The monster gurgled and quickly melted back to the puddle of gloop that it had come from. Poor monster. 'Make me a better one, Igon. And make it really evil this time.'

She swept out of the room like a new broom.

My walking stick wasn't laughing

Edna Crudge was a dragon of a woman. No, that's unfair. Unfair to dragons.

She had a fierce face that said, 'Do as I say,' or, 'If you don't give up your seat on the bus to me then I'll breathe on you and singe your eyebrows till they're black and smoking, twirling, crumbling ash.'

When she walked down the street the traffic wardens of Wildpool town ran and hid in shop doorways. People said that her first husband had dropped down dead in the vegetable garden: the first she knew of the tragedy was when a neighbour rattled on her kitchen door and sobbed, 'Oh, Edna, your Arthur has dropped down dead in the cabbage patch.'

'What a nuisance,' Edna said with a shake of her head. 'He was supposed to be cutting a cabbage for our Sunday dinner.'

'Oh, Edna, what will you do?' the neighbour howled[2].

'What'll I do?' Edna growled. 'I suppose I'll just have to open a can of peas.'

The dead husband was buried ... but not in the cabbage patch ... and Edna married that neighbour: Billy Crudge.

'She's one in a million,' Billy said.

'A million what? Bulldogs?' Billy's dad asked, sour as old vinegar. 'Did you know, yesterday, I was walking down Wildpool High Street and she kicked my walking stick from under me? She said I didn't need a walking stick.'

'She's right, Dad,' Billy said with a chuckle.

'That's not the point,' the old man moaned. 'I should have smacked her on her head with my stick.'

2 To be honest a neighbour doesn't howl like a wolf. A neighbour neighs ... like a horse. That's why they're called neigh-bours. By the way, that story about a first husband wasn't true. She only ever had one husband and that was Billy the Caretaker Crudge.

'Why didn't you?' Billy asked.

'Because she'd kicked the stick into the middle of the road and a car ran over it.'

'You have to laugh,' Billy said. And he did.

'My walking stick wasn't laughing,' Dad grumbled.

Forty years passed, as years usually do, until Edna Crudge was a member of a fearsome threesome of old ladies. They met every day at the Top Coffee Café, opposite Loaf Tower. They watched the world of Wildpool pass by. And when they saw a wrong they righted it. And sometimes they saw things that weren't wrong ... but they righted *those* a little bit more.

Villains and desperadoes of Wildpool walked in fear of the Three Just Women.

Edna's friends were the limp Marjorie Doors and the little Minnie Cooper. Marjorie had a black belt in knitting. Minnie was wirier than a barbed-wire fence and tougher than she looked.

But one misty morning she didn't look as tough as barbed tissue paper. She held a letter in her trembling hand. She didn't say a word. She just passed it across for Edna and Marjorie to read.

I is gone and is
never coming back

Let us turn the clock back a week … no, I don't mean push the pointers back 7 times 24 hours[3]. I mean let's think about what happened a week ago that upset Minnie Cooper now.

It began with a notice outside Wildpool Town Hall.

New mayor of Wildpool
selected today at 10 a.m.
on the Town Square.
Be there.

---

3 And as you know, 7 times 24 equals … an awful lot of hours. And even more minutes and a stupendous number of seconds.

The people gathered. Ten stone steps led up to the pillars of the grand Town Hall. On the top step was a large wooden box. Beside the box there was a small man, dressed in black and wearing an eyepatch. His name struck terror into the hearts of every stray dog in Wildpool. It was Igon – the town's most brilliant scientist, and Wildpool's dog-catcher in his spare time.

He cleared his throat. 'Ahem. Ladies and gentlemen of Wildpool, we are here today to pick the next mayor of Wildpool. The name of every adult living in Wildpool is in this box. I will pull one name out. That person will be mayor till the day they die.'

'The old mayor isn't dead,' a woman with a shopping bag called out.

'No but he has disappeared, never to be seen again,' Igon said.

'How do you know?' a tall man with a bad haircut shouted. He was a schoolteacher and he was used to shouting.

'He left a note,' Igon said, and pulled a piece of paper from his pocket. '"I is gone and is never coming back not never not no-how."'

The teacher shook his head. 'He was always hopeless at English. I was his teacher, you know. Couldn't spell to save his life.'

'Why can't we vote? Make sure we get the person we want?' Mrs Shopping-Bag asked.

'It is an old charter for the town written in 1493 when King Henry VIII passed a law saying Wildpool mayor is chosen by a lottery.'

The teacher sighed. 'Henry VIII was just two years old that year.'

'And a very clever boy for his age,' Igon argued. 'Now please allow me to draw the winner... I mean, the name of the new mayor of Wildpool.'

A girl watched the man in black plunge his hand into the box. She had red-gold hair in a long plait. She turned to the boy next to her. He was as thin as a schoolbook but twice as clever. 'It's a trick, Boy,' she said.

'Yes, Molly,' Boy replied. 'Igon has a slip of paper tucked into his watchstrap. He'll pull it out and read the name he wrote on it an hour ago.'

'How do you know?' she asked.

'Because I'm a trickster and a thief. It's what I'd do,' he said with a shrug.

The man with the eyepatch pulled out a slip of paper and waved it above his head. He didn't even bother to read it.

'I have the honour of naming the new mayor of Wildpool,' he said with a grim and gap-toothed smile. (A smile ... but a baleful one. A shifty, devious, guilty smile that said, 'You DO believe me ... don't you?' No, Igon. We *DON'T*.)

Forty dirty, cramped and crumbly houses

Now let's get back to the present day – seven days after the new mayor of Wildpool was announced. Edna screwed up her eyes to read the letter Minnie Cooper handed to her. She read it aloud for Marjorie to hear.

'"Dear House owner," it says. "We are pleased to tell you that you will be moving to a nice new home."'

'I don't want a nice new home,' Minnie muttered. 'I've lived in that old one for seventy years. I was born there.'

Edna read on.

'"Wildpool Council is planning to knock down all the houses in Pump Street. There are just forty dirty, cramped and crumbly houses and shops and they should have been knocked down years ago."'

'My house may be small,' Minnie said, 'but it's big enough for me. And I keep it clean as a polished pin.'

Edna's face turned dragon dark.

'"There are empty council houses on Wildpool's Blackbird Hill and we will make sure you can move into one by the end of the month."'

'Blackbird Hill's not a nice place,' Marjorie said, and her knitting needles flew so fast they could have sparked a Girl Scout's fire into life. 'Young men race fast cars around the streets. Bored kids play loud music all night, the gardens are wild as jungles and the pavements are cracked.'

'I don't want to go there,' Minnie moaned and trembled.

Edna blew out her cheeks. 'You won't,' she told her friend. 'I have a house down the road. I let young people stay there. There's always room.'

Marjorie Doors rapped the table with her

knitting needles. 'Those young people in your house are *thieves*, Edna. You teach them how to steal and they go out robbing the people of Wildpool like . . . like. . .'

'Like Robin Hood,' Edna said angrily. 'We only rob the rich so we can look after the poor. And I save the young people from that terrible orphanage.'

Marjorie was surprised to find herself growling at Edna. It was something she'd never dared to do before. 'You can*not* expect Minnie to live in a den of thieves. No. Listen. She has her lovely little house in Pump Street. There's no reason for her to move. Not to Blackbird Hill. Not to your house of thieves.'

Edna was shocked. Not many people argued with her. 'No reason, you say, Marjorie Doors? No reason? Well there's the reason. Here in this letter. They are going to build a new road. A new, wide road through the middle of the town. It says here it will bring people into the shops of Wildpool from miles around. The shops in Wildpool will be better off.'

'We have shops in Pump Street,' Minnie

sighed. 'My friends that own the shops won't be better off. Their shops will be flattened.'

Tears began to fill Minnie's faded eyes. Edna took a deep breath. 'Very well. If you don't want to move from Pump Street, then don't move[4].'

'But the road...'

'We'll stop them building it,' Edna said.

'But we can't stop Wildpool Council, Edna. Have you seen who signed that letter?'

'I don't care,' Edna said, fierce as a fox in a farmyard.

'Who signed it?' Marjorie Doors asked.

Edna held out the letter. 'The mayor of Wildpool. That's who. The new mayor of Wildpool.'

---

4 Can they make Minnie move? Always remember: you can drag a horse to water but a pencil must be lead.

People will flock to wonderful Wildpool

Of course, I am forgetting. You don't know who this mayor of Wildpool is, do you? I wound you back in time then wound you forward again. Your winding spring is going to snap if we keep doing that.

So, Igon the eyepatched man-in-black said, 'I have the honour of naming the new mayor of Wildpool.'

The people in the crowd held their breath. No one said, 'Let it be me, please let it be me.' No one said that … but everybody thought it.

'The new mayor is … Lady Mary Frankenstone.'

The crowd groaned[5]. The lady with the shopping bag gave a choking cry. Boy, the thief, turned to Molly. 'I told you it was fixed.'

The lady with the shopping bag sobbed, 'Somebody's nicked my purse from my bag.'

Edna Crudge moved towards Boy, reached into his pocket and pulled out the purse. She dropped it on the ground. 'Oh, look, lady. Is this your purse? You must have dropped it.'

'Ah, you're a life-saver,' the woman sighed.

Edna glared at Boy and hissed, 'We rob from the *rich* to give to the *poor*. Behave, Boy. We are on the side of the good.'

Boy looked ashamed. 'Lady Greystone isn't good,' he muttered as the new mayor stepped from the crowd and walked to the top of the steps with a wide smile on her face. 'Lady Greystone may have changed her name to Frankenstone, but she's still a thief and a kidnapper. She kidnapped Molly here. She should be behind bars.'

Molly shook her head. 'No. The evil Arfur Loaf kidnapped me *for* Lady Greystone, but I'm not sure the police can put the blame on her.'

'People of Wildpool,' Lady Frankenstone

---

5 Though some muttered, 'Oh, dear,' and others said, 'Lady Mary Who?'

cried in a voice that rang as loud as Wildpool Town Hall's clock chimes. 'It is such an honour. I promise you I will serve you faithfully and turn Wildpool into a rich and beautiful town. People will flock to wonderful Wildpool. I have great plans for this town.'

'How can you have great plans when you were elected mayor just one minute ago?' a man in a flat cap asked.

'Good question,' Boy said, 'but we know the answer.'

Lady Mary Frankenstone gazed up to the sooty spires and tottering towers of the town. Her bleached hair blew in the wind and her red dress fluttered like a flag on the beach that meant, 'No swimming.'

'I have a dream,' she cried.

'A nightmare,' Edna Crudge muttered. And, as usual, she was right.

Shabby shows of shocks and shadows

Lady Frankenstone waved a hand at the tawdry town behind her. 'I am the owner of Frankenstone Castle ... that fine old stately home on the hill.'

'I thought it was called Greystone Castle,' the tall man with a bad haircut shouted in the voice that school-teachers usually use.

The woman in red gave him a glare and a strained smile. 'The Normans originally named it Frankenstone when they invaded in 1077—'

'1066,' the teacher cried. Everyone knows that.'

'The Normans didn't get to Wildpool till 1077,' she explained.

'That's not in my history books,' the tall man said, and his bad haircut sprang into spikes of annoyance.

'Then you are reading the wrong history books,' Lady Frankenstone said in a voice like washed gravel. 'I found an ancient book when I bought the castle ... *Frankenstone* Castle. It says the Normans changed the name when they finally crushed the brave Romans of Wildpool.

The teacher just shook his head and gave up[6].

'My dream is to turn Frankenstone Castle into a new attraction for tourists. I will fill it with fantastic and frightening scenes and moving models that are so real they will scare you witless.'

'Ooooh,' the crowd gasped.

'Wiggott's Wonderful Waxworld tried that and it closed down years ago,' the woman with a shopping bag sneered. 'It was too scary.'

'It was a dusty old trail through shabby shows of shocks and shadows,' Lady Frankenstone sighed. 'Mine will be spectacular and up to date.'

6 You will be pleased about that. You do NOT want a lecture on history, do you? You DO? Then go and read a Horrible Histories book. They're rather good.

'Well, I'll go and see it,' the woman with the shopping bag said.

'I will smarten up the old Wildpool docks. Pleasure cruisers will land with happy families and they will be swept in self-drive buses through Wildpool to my castle on the hill.'

'That'll take them ages in the twisted tangle of Wildpool's streets,' the man in a flat cap argued.

Lady Frankenstone gave a wide grin and for once she looked really happy. 'That is why I plan to build a wide new road that will run from the docks to the castle. Frankenstone Highway.'

'You'd have to knock down Pump Street to build that road,' Edna Crudge said in a voice with all the heat of a dragon's breath. 'My friend Minnie was born there and she's lived there seventy years.'

'Awwww,' the crowd sighed.

'Then it's time she had a change ... and a change is as good as a rest. Orders will go out next week.'

The crowd were glum and silent. Igon stepped forward and punched the air with his fist. Luckily, the air didn't punch him back.

'Three cheers for Mayor Frankenstone and her dream to make Wildpool great again. Hip-hip...'

'Hooray,' a young policeman shouted ... but that was the only voice in the stale air of the old town square. The rest of the crowd were drifting away and muttering, 'I liked old Wiggott's Wonderful Waxworld.'

I could lie down in front of the bulldozers

'So, this evil woman is going to put Wiggott's permanently out of business AND destroy Minnie's home,' Edna Crudge said.

'She has to be stopped,' Marjorie Doors paused in her knitting to sip coffee at the Top Coffee Café.

'I could lie down in front of the bulldozers,' timid Minnie Cooper said. Timidly.

Edna looked at her friend with pity. 'Minnie. Marjorie here has just done your hair. When the bulldozers run over you they will ruin that new hairstyle. Marjorie here will be very upset. Won't you, Marjorie?'

'I will, Edna. Took me an hour to do Minnie's hair. Wouldn't want to see it wasted.'

Minnie's small mouth went tight. 'Thank you for that, Marjorie. I won't forget that.'

Edna snorted. 'You forget most things these days, Minnie.'

The timid Minnie clamped her lips tight. The three women supped their coffees in silence for a while and turned their eyes on Loaf Tower. The great glass tower in the middle of Wildpool town stood out like a diamond in a dustbin. Wildpool had twisted streets of smoked-brown buildings and narrow alleys as dark as the inky river that ran under the black-brick bridges[7]. The tower was new and sparkling in the sun that flitted through the fire-fogged air.

Three old women looked out through the dust-stained window. The kind people of Wildpool called them the Ladies Who Crunch. (The unkind people called them the three witches.)

A girl strode up the road towards them with the boy-thief called Boy shuffling along behind her, looking for danger and looking to rob like

---

7 Oh, it's easy enough for me to write 'black-brick bridges', but you just try SAYING it out loud. Your tongue could be twisted in knots for hours. Or days. Don't try it at home.

Robin. They entered the café and sat at the table of the Ladies Who Crunch. 'You should be at school, young Molly Maltby.'

The red-haired girl jerked a thumb at Boy. '*He* isn't.'

Edna sniffed. 'Boy is learning at the University of Life.'

Molly gave a sweet smile as false as the bottom of a magician's cabinet. 'Then I'll join his university for a few days. You need my help. . .'

'Our help,' Boy muttered.

Molly gave a short nod. 'You need *our* help. We've heard there's a new attraction at the castle. Boy did a lot to help Dr Wiggott save his Waxworld before. It's due to reopen next month, they say. But Frankenstone Castle will finish the good Dr Wiggott's Waxworld off for good.'

Boy's eyes burned with a strange energy. 'And put your husband out of job, Mrs Crudge. We also heard about the plans to flatten Pump Street. We need a plan to save them both. You three ladies make the best plans in the history of the world.'

'Well, the history of Wildpool,' Molly corrected him.

Edna took in a deep breath. 'Firstly, we need to know what's going on inside Loaf Tower. Molly, can you get in there and spy for us?'

The girl gasped. 'Edna... I was held prisoner in there by the evil Arfur Loaf. I never want to go back again.'

'Good point.' Marjorie nodded.

'What do you suggest, Marjorie Mastermind?' Edna huffed.

'Let Boy go into Loaf Tower and let Molly go to Wiggott's Wonderful Waxworld to see what Dr Wiggott plans.'

Edna shrugged. 'Dr Wiggott isn't there at the moment... but my husband Billy, the Waxworld caretaker, may be able to help.'

And so, the plan was made in two minutes and fourteen seconds. The Ladies Who Crunch really were the best plot-planners in the history of Wildpool.

Will remain on watch in case she is kidnapped again

Molly Maltby slipped into the sunless cavern that she knew as Dank Alley. You won't find it on any town map. Put it into a smartphone map app and it will say, 'No such place. Check your spelling.' Or, 'Get your eyes tested.'

Yet *Dank Alley* was chalked on the wall at the entrance. Maybe it was a warning? 'This is a dank alley – wear rubber boots.' Rubber boots would have kept the water from the damp cobbles out of the girl's trainers. 'Boy didn't warn me about the slime and the wet,' she grumbled.

Somewhere rats laughed at her, then disappeared down their rat-holes to the sewers below ground.

The tall walls of the alley were of warped wood and soot-stained stone. The cobbles glowed with their own green light and were slippery underfoot. Molly was looking down at her feet, so she could place them carefully. She was angry with Boy. She was not looking over her shoulder[8]. If she had been, she'd have seen she was being watched.

Most of the old doors in the alley walls were cobwebbed shut and had no sign to say what lay behind. She stepped deeper into the gloom. At last she came across a sign under a glowing gas lamp.

Once it had said *Wiggott's Wonderful Waxworld* in glistening gold letters. Underneath even fainter writing said: *Deliveries – Knock three times.*

She rapped with her knuckles. *Knock – knock – knock.*

The door creaked open and an old man

---

8 Well you can't, can you? You can look forward angrily at the dangers ahead. But you can't look back in anger. Not at the same time.

peered out. The caretaker's face was thin as his body and still thinner wisps of hair clung to his shining head. 'Edna phoned to say you were on your way,' he said. 'How can I help you?'

'There's a new attraction opening at Frankenstone Castle in a few days' time. Will Dr Wiggott's Wonderful Waxworld be open before then?'

The old man scratched his chin. 'I don't think so. I'm working twelve hours every day, but I've only finished one scene ... the Great Fire of Rome ... and that's taken me two weeks. I started it soon after that boy-thief delivered the infinit-G microchip. Come into the workshop and I'll show you.'

Molly followed Billy Crudge through a musty corridor and into a large workshop. One wall was covered in flashing computer panels, monitors and lights in more colours than the rainbow. It was clean as a safety pin.

A table stood in the middle of the room with a large metal tank hanging over it. Billy Crudge opened a valve under the tank and let out a bucket of gloop. It was a shimmering blob of slime. 'The infinit-G chip can turn this stuff into any character from the history of the world,' he said. 'It looks as real as a human. The infinit-G does all the research so the brain of the character knows everything about itself. Here, I'll show you. This is the last character we need for the Roman scene.' He looked at the gloop and spoke. 'Infinit-G ... make me a Waxworld character of Emperor Nero from ancient Rome.'

The computers hummed. (Maybe they didn't know the words.) Lights sparked across the panels and words sped over the screens. The gloop began to tremble like rice pudding on a railway track when the express train to Wildpool was fifty metres away. The gloop began to change shape. It began to look like a large jelly-baby...

Outside on the slippery cobbles a policeman muttered softly into his radio. 'PC L.O. Elloe reporting. The girl Molly Maltby is inside the Waxworld. Safe and well. Will remain on watch in case she is kidnapped again. Over.'

There was a faint crackle and a groan.
'Stop whispering, Elloe. I can't hear you.'

'Sorry,' PC Elloe whispered.

Have you heard the news? The incredibly amazing news?

Meanwhile, at the underground entrance to Loaf Tower, Boy marched up to the heavy steel door and pushed the buzzer. After a moment a voice replied sounding like a tin man who'd swallowed a bucket of empty cans. 'Can I help you?'

Boy knew there was a camera watching him and put on his most excited face as if he'd just won the lottery jackpot as his deadliest enemy tripped headfirst into a bucket of pigswill.

'Hi. Hi. Have you heard the news? The incredibly amazing news?'

The door clicked and swung open. A security guard stood there. He was too large for his navy uniform and his round face was as pink as a pink carnation[9]. His badge said...

BRIAN
Here to help

'Who are you then?' the guard asked. This was a very sensible question from a man with a very stupid face.

'I'm Lady Greystone's personal assistant, Brian,' Boy said.

'Who's she?'

'Sorry, sorry, sorry,' the young thief moaned. If his leg had been long enough he'd have kicked himself.

'Frankenstone, I mean. Lady Frankenstone.'

'Ah, the boss-lady. You work for her, do you? I've never seen you around here before.'

---

9 If everyone in the country owned a pink car, would this be a pink car-nation? Just wondering.

'I've never been here before. I work up at Frankenstone Castle,' he lied. 'I write all her emails, look after her business affairs and the people who work for her. People like you, Brian.'

The eyes in the round, pink face grew wide. 'You look a bit young to do all that.'

Boy leaned forward and said, 'I'm a genius. Far too clever for my age. But I can see you are nearly as clever, Brian ... Brian Brainbox, we call you up at the castle. When I get back to the castle I will tell her ladyship to give you a pay rise.'

'Really?'

'Really. I know how much she pays you and I will tell her to pay you double, because you are so good at this job. No one – I mean *no* one – will get into Loaf Tower while you are on guard here. Her ladyship and me – well, we rely on loyal and trusty, brave and clever, strong and handsome people like you.'

'Handsome?'

'Handsome as a bulldog with three legs. Now, if you'll show me to Lady Frankenstone's office, Brian, I'll collect her notes and tell her how helpful you have been.'

The guard raised a hand to his podgy head in a salute. 'Of course, sir. Walk this way.'

Ten minutes later Boy left the building with two carrier bags stuffed with files marked *infinit-G*, *microchips*, *smartphones* and *memory cards*. There was even a glossy sheet of paper printed with an advert for the new Frankenstone Castle attraction.

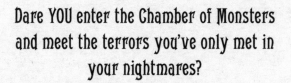

Dare YOU enter the Chamber of Monsters and meet the terrors you've only met in your nightmares?

Forget old Waxworld.

Frankenstone Castle's creations are so REAL you will have HORRORS to make your hair stand on end.

(Bald men will be supplied with wigs.)

'Forget Wiggott's?' Boy muttered as he walked past the guard. 'We'll see. We'll see.' He looked up and smiled at the large man in the tight blue uniform. 'I do hope you don't get the sack,' he said.

Brian the guard turned a little green. As Boy disappeared into the murky streets of Wildpool, Brian had a sudden feeling he'd done something very wrong. Very wrong and very stupid.

Oh, dear.

There's no place like Rome

Molly stepped onto the little railway carriage on a narrow track that ran into twisting ribbon of faint blue light. The Emperor Nero sat in the front seat alongside Billy Crudge. The Waxworld model's face was set like a statue. And the hazel eyes stared ahead – haughty, proud ... and just a little mad.

The room had the gloom of a doom-filled tomb. Blue bulbs like glow-worms sparkled in the high ceiling but they only gave a faint light.

The electric train whirred and clanked over the rusting rails. It ran slowly through the tomb-gloom-room. At each turn there was a new scene for the passenger to view.

Dust-covered wax figures stood in painted wooden scenes from the past. As you rattled towards ancient Rome you would find yourself in the Wild West of America, now in a dungeon from the Middle Ages and now face-to-face with a villainous Victorian.

A historical tour of every age and a dozen countries. They had just one thing the same: the figures were wax models of the evillest people who ever lived. The matted hair and rotting clothes on the sawdust-stuffed bodies, the shabby scenes and the paint-peeling walls all looked harmless enough. But you should never look at the eyes.

The glass eyes in the wicked wax faces glittered in the green light on the front of the electric train. The eyes would seem to follow you on your train trip. They would watch you come, and watch you go. It was almost as if they wished they could get their wax hands around your... But enough. Stop before you scare me.

This is Wiggott's Wonderful Waxworld.

A crumbling old building on the outside – boarded up at the front with peeling posters saying, *Sorry we've closed*. The back door, in the dimness of Dank Alley, was the only way in. Not many people made their way down the rat-infested cobbles to that old warped door. When the glittering attraction of Frankenstone's Castle opened, then Wiggott's Wonderful Waxworld would never see another visitor.

Molly rode on past the derelict scenes while, outside, a bicycle stood in the alley. A label on the saddle said, *Police Property. Do not steal. By order of PC L.O. Elloe*. But there was no sign of PC Elloe[10].

There was a crackle and a hiss. The girl thought the train was making the noise. But it was the ancient speakers in the run-down Waxworld sparking into life. 'Visitors, please stay on the train. It is forbidden to step off the trains at any time. This could be very dangerous.'

Molly leaned forward. 'What's that noise?' she asked.

'The Waxworld sound system,' the balding man explained. 'It cuts in every five minutes.'

10 So you could couldn't say, 'Hello, L.O. Elloe.' But you could say, 'Hello, Elloe's bike.'

'Is it really dangerous to step off the train?' the girl asked.

'Not any more. The old animatronic figures have been switched off. We'll replace them with the infinit-G models. Let's put Nero in his place and see how it all works. This is the most important day in Wiggott's Wonderful Waxworld for fifty years,' Billy said, and the train creaked to a halt beside a scene showing men and women in togas and tunics.

Billy grinned at the figure beside him. 'Here we are, Nero, my old mate. Ancient Rome. There's no place like home ... hurr, hurr ... or should I say there's no place like Rome?'

The infinit-G figure looked at the caretaker as if he was a bad smell and hissed, 'I am not your mate.' The figure of Nero looked at the calm, still scene and cried, 'My people, bow down! Your Emperor Nero is arrived.'

Billy sighed. 'The infinit-G figure doesn't just *look* like Nero. He *acts* like the real Nero too.'

'He was a bit of a nutter,' Molly sighed.

'Just a bit,' Billy agreed.

Bears and lions rip off your flesh

Molly, Billy Crudge and Nero got off the train and found themselves in a hot, dusty Rome. The emperor stepped forward and snatched a flat musical instrument from the hands of a skinny servant standing immobile nearby. It was like a wooden pudding bowl with strings across. The label on the scene read...

Emperor Nero. 18 July, AD 64. Nero fiddles while Rome burns.

'That's not a fiddle,' Molly argued.

'Lyre, girl. Lyre,' Billy Crudge hissed.

The girl glared at him. 'Don't call me a liar.'

The caretaker sighed. 'L-Y-R-E ... lyre. Fiddles weren't invented in ancient Rome. They say Nero played a lyre while the city burned.'

'Why would he do that?' Molly wondered. 'Wait a moment and I'll check.' She pressed the screen of her phone. Moments later, she said, 'Here we are ... it says that Emperor Nero wanted buildings in Rome cleared so he could build a fine palace. The people of Rome refused. A fire broke out on 18 July, AD 64. Many people think Nero started the fire then played music as he watched the flames. Other reports say he was fifty miles away and he couldn't have started it. It's a mystery.'

'Puh,' Billy snorted. 'We haven't time to solve mysteries. We have to see how the infinit-G works ... if it's safer than the old Waxworld figures.'

'And if it's not?' Molly asked.

Billy shrugged. 'Then we could all be in danger.'

'Great,' the girl sighed. She took one step forward, past the figure of the evil emperor who was beginning to stroke the strings of his lyre.

The warmth and the smell of the street grew stronger. She took a second step. The painted wooden floor under her feet felt like sandy stone paving. The figures on the street were stirring into life.

When Molly looked back the Roman figures were moving. Moving slowly at first as if they had been stuck there with treacle. Now they were struggling free. Their movements grew faster till they were running freely down the street. Nero was lost in the crowd now. Molly thought flickering red on the sleeves of the Romans were flames from the Great Fire. The Roman crowd were screaming.

When she looked back there was no Wiggott's Wonderful Waxworld railway line, just the crowded streets of a sun-baked city. People were hurrying past her and crying out. The red streams from their sleeves were bright ribbons.

The screams weren't fear of fire but howls of happiness. A chubby woman stopped for breath, the sweat on her face running like the ribbons she wore.

'Where's the fire?' Molly asked.

The woman grinned a crack-toothed grin. 'By Jupiter, there's no fire,' she laughed and waddled on. Molly hurried after her.

'So why is everyone running away?'

'They aren't running *away*, mutton-brain ... they are running to the Circus,' the woman said as she puffed and wheezed like a pair of broken bellows.

'A circus? With clowns?' Molly asked.

The woman frowned. 'You are *very* stupid ... or you are a Celt[11] ... and if you are a Celt you're a slave and should be with your master. I'll report you to the Emperor's Guard. You know what will happen then?'

'Tell me,' Molly muttered.

'They will take you to the arena and tie you to a stake while bears and lions rip off your flesh. Rome is a dangerous place for Celts,' she hissed.

'Oh, Mr Crudge,' Molly moaned. 'What have you let me in for?'

Billy Crudge didn't answer. Billy Crudge wasn't there.

---

11 Of course, she could be *both*. A stupid Celt. She never thought of that. But neither did you.

Red-red-red, soon be dead

Agang of sweating, red-faced men swept Molly along the road. One of them grabbed her arm and tied a red ribbon around her wrist. The man's wrinkled, fun-filled face was a little kinder than the others. 'There you go, lass, heh. Safer if you wear that.'

'Safer?'

'Safer, heh, if you support the reds when you're in the red part of town.'

They were half-running down the street in the midst of a babbling bubble of people, all wearing red ribbons. 'What are the ribbons for?' she asked.

'You're not a Celt, are you, girl, eh, heh?' the old man asked.

'No,' the girl said quickly.

'Red ribbons show you support the red team, see, heh? Not the blues or the whites ... and especially not the greens,' the man explained.

'What teams?'

The man sighed. 'The chariot teams. You're off to the Circus Maximus, aren't you, heh? You're going to watch the chariots race? You have to support one of the teams, don't you?'

'I was just looking for Nero,' she said.

'You can find him after the races. He'll be there,' the old man chuckled. 'But with a few thousand Romans there you may have trouble spotting him, heh?'

Molly let herself be rushed along. They turned a corner and ahead of them was a vast wooden building, twice as long as the football arena where the Wanderers football team played in Wildpool[12].

Suddenly there were angry shouts and the crowds began to swirl like a whirlpool.

12 The Romans didn't play football, of course. Poor Romans. They may not have been so cruel if they'd had football. They'd not have shouted, 'Kill the Christians!' More likely to shout, 'Julius full-back, mark Antony!'

Men with green ribbons on their wrists or round their heads blocked the way and jeered and spat at Molly's red crowd. There was no fighting but a lot of hatred.

There was quite a bit of pushing and insults thrown around. A lad of Molly's age ran up to her and squealed in her face, 'Red-red-red, soon be dead.'

She glared back and shouted, 'Green-green-green ... erm ... eat my jeans.'

The lad blinked. 'Eh? What's that supposed to mean?'

She shrugged. 'Dunno. I just thought of it.'

'Greens are the emperor's team. You can't talk to me like that,' the lad said.

'I just did,' Molly said, pleased with herself. She saw a wide door in the wooden walls of the Circus Maximus open into the cool darkness beneath the stands. As she made for it she felt a bony claw of a hand grip her shoulder.

'There you are, girl. I've been looking for you.' Molly wriggled but couldn't get free.

A woman with snakes for hair

B oy ran across to the Top Coffee Café where the Ladies Who Crunch were waiting with cold, empty cups.

Boy spread his stolen treasures on the table and they shared out the files. At last Edna Crudge said, 'They are not going to show scenes from history, the way the great Dr Wiggott does.'

Marjorie Doors nodded. 'They are going to show monsters from books and stories.'

Boy tapped a sheet of paper. 'It looks like they've already created Frankenstein's monster ... but it failed. It didn't have the monster's mad brain. It looked horrible, but it wasn't scary at all.'

Minnie Cooper said, 'So, they had the infinit-G but don't know how to use it? Dr Wiggott has time to catch up ... make exciting scenes from history so that visitors can learn as they ride around. Schoolteachers will love that. The place will be packed. Well done, Boy.'

But Boy wasn't listening. He was reading a report. 'Oh,' was all he said.

'What?' the Ladies Who Crunch asked.

'They tried to make Frankenstein's monster again. Each time they tried they made a cheerful, friendly creature. I saw it in Loaf Tower. It'll come back to life at the flick of a switch. Then they made Count Dracula, a werewolf, a one-eyed Cyclops...'

'That's from the Greek legends,' Marjorie Doors said wisely, and took up her knitting again.

'A Gorgon...'

'A woman with snakes for hair.'

'And a zombie,' Boy finished.

'Sounds like fun,' Minnie Cooper said. The others glared at her. 'Sorry,' she muttered.

'But they all turned out too cheerful,' Boy said, reading on.

'So, they melted them back into gloop and planned to start again?' Edna Crudge said. 'That's what Dr Wiggott would do.'

'No...' Boy said, turning the page. 'It seems they dressed them up in modern clothes. Only Frankenstone's monster was left behind.' He found another printed sheet. 'And here's an order to take them to the Town Hall at ten o'clock today.'

'Nonsense,' Edna snapped. 'That doesn't make sense.' She snatched the paper from Boy and read it for herself. 'Well, yes, it says that,' she agreed. 'But why would Lady Mary Frankenstone want to fill the Town Hall with her monsters?'

Minnie gave a gentle cough. 'It's five minutes to ten now, Edna. We could always go and find out.'

Edna snorted angrily – angry because she hadn't thought of that for herself. 'Another of your mad ideas, Minnie.'

'Do you have a better idea, Edna?'

'Yes,' Edna said, and she slapped the table till

the coffee cups rattled. 'After all, as Boy said, the Ladies Who Crunch make the best plans in the world. So, I suggest we go to the Town Hall and find out what Lady Frankenstone is up to.'

They had four minutes to reach the Town Hall, four hundred metres away. Would they make it in time[13]?

13 Don't ask me. I don't know how fast elderly ladies can run/shuffle/walk and I haven't the time to find out. I am much too busy telling the true story of Wiggott's Wonderful Waxworld.

Fuff-er fuff-a-fuff er fuff nng-fuff

B oy reached the Town Hall first, as you'd expect. He pushed through the heavy oak doors and into the council hall. On a platform at the far end of the room sat the woman in the red dress and red shoes. Her legs were stretched out in front of her and showed that even the soles of her shoes were red ... and Boy (like me) never knew why.

Behind the new mayor there was a map of Wildpool, projected onto a screen. The twisting roads wound round enough to make a lost driver dizzy.

The room was crowded with people who were angry, people who were curious and people who didn't know why they were there but wanted to see why everyone else was there.

'Ladies and gentlemen,' Lady Frankenstone said, 'there has been a fire alarm in the building. I'm afraid I must ask you to leave.'

A great groan arose from the crowd and cross or curious people shambled and scuffled, waddled and trundled out. But, as Boy watched from the back of the room, five people stayed in their seats. They wore large hats and coats with the collars turned up. What were they hiding, you ask? Wait and see, I reply.

'Now we can begin the meeting,' Lady Frankenstone said with a red-lipped smile. 'I am the mayor and it is my honour to present to you my new plan for Wildpool.'

The five shady figures clapped their hands and gave a croaking, rasping, growling, squawking, cawing cheer. It sounded more like feeding time at the zoo. The door swung open and the Ladies Who Crunch shuffled in and took their seats in the front row. Boy sat beside them.

Lady Frankenstone glared. 'Is that everyone?' she asked.

'Yes,' Edna Crudge said.

'Then I'm all right,' the new mayor said with a small smile. She clicked a button and the picture on the screen changed. It was still a map of Wildpool. But now, where the roads had twisted dizzily there was a wide blue line straight from the docks to the castle on the hill. And some of the houses had gone. All of Pump Street had been swallowed.

'Here is my plan for the new road,' her ladyship announced. 'All those in favour, raise their hands.' Five secret figures raised their hands and gave a squeaking cheer. 'All those against?' The Ladies Who Crunch (and Boy) raised their hands. The mayor beamed. 'My plan is carried by five votes to four.'

Minnie cried, 'You've flattened my house. It's not fair.'

'It isn't raining, heh, heh,' hissed a voice from behind her. The ladies turned around and saw that underneath the wide hat was a woman with eyes of evil and snakes that writhed out from under the brim where her hair should be.

'Fuff-er fuff-a-fuff er fuff nng-fuff,' a man in a dark cape croaked. Fangs glowed like ivory from the corners of his mouth.

'He said it's a great plan,' a friend beside him said. The man had a face as hairy as a wolf and hairy paws poked out of his coat sleeves. 'He can't speak very well with those teeth, can you, Count Dracula?'

'Fuff-er fuff-a-fuff er fuff nng-fuff.'

'Durrrrr,' a zombie roared.

'It's a lovely plan,' a huge man with one eye in the middle of his forehead giggled. 'Lovely idea. And such a pretty map. It even has a cycle lane for us Cyclops ... a sort of cycle-op-lane. Great.'

'Then the road shall be built,' the mayor said.

'No-o-o-o,' moaned Minnie. But Lady Frankenstone wasn't listening. She was speaking into her phone.

'So, Igon, when will the demolition team be ready to start on Pump Street? This morning? Great... What? A robbery? There has been a robbery at Loaf Tower? And my plans for the Chamber of Monsters have been stolen? I'll be back right away.'

She glared at the monsters in the council room. She opened an app on her phone and pressed a button. *Bleep.* There was a gurgle and soon five hats sat on top of five puddles of gloop[14].

'Can we have another vote now?' Marjorie Doors called out. But the mayor had slithered off faster than a red herring.

14 Yes, I know. She has destroyed her own creations. Why? Because she thought she could make new ones as soon as she got back to Loaf Tower. But Boy had stolen the infinit-G chip. A lesson for us there: look before you bleep.

Halt, in the
name of Plod

PC Laurence Olivier Elloe – or L.O. Elloe as they called him at the police station – had marched up and down Dank Alley twelve times. One for every day of the week, then another for a week with Saturday and Sunday off. (Even a plodding police constable deserves a day off now and then.)

At last, he checked the chain that fastened his bike to a railing. He checked the buttons on his uniform were shining. He looked in a glistening puddle to make sure his helmet was straight. He marched up to the back door of

Wiggott's Wonderful Waxworld, where a sign said, *Knock three times*.

Knock-knock-knock.

Nothing happened. 'Old Mr Crudge is usually in his office by the door,' he said to himself. He knew what he had to do. His knees began to tremble at the very thought. But he did it. He drew his truncheon from his belt and smashed it on the door as hard as he could. The old, damp, warped wood crumbled around the ancient lock and the door swung open. 'Oo-er,' he gasped, shocked by his own courage in attacking a seventy-year-old door[15].

He stepped into the musty gloom. The blue lights twinkled in the ceiling like stars that had been there from the beginning of time. 'Hello? Mr Crudge? Are you there?'

Mr Crudge didn't reply. Maybe he didn't reply because he *wasn't* there. Or because he was deaf. Or dead. PC Elloe tiptoed to the small room where the caretaker spent a lot of his time.

There was a half-eaten sausage sandwich on

---

15 That was harmless enough. But we should worry if he used his truncheon to attack your old, damp, warped granny. Which I'm sure no police officer would ever do.

the table beside a cold cup of tea. Abandoned by Billy Crudge. PC Elloe had always wanted to be a detective. He'd read every book that Agatha Christie had written ... and a lot of Enid Blyton books too. (His favourite character was Mr Plod the Policeman. Plod often caught the villains on his police bicycle, by blowing his whistle and shouting, 'Halt, in the name of Plod!' before locking them up in his jail. And Mr Plod would have looked at the cold tea and sausage sandwich and said, 'Aha! Mr Crudge was disturbed in the middle of eating his breakfast.' And Plodding Constable Elloe would have been right. Brilliant detective work.)

Mr Plod was the reason PC Elloe joined the police force. He was just sad that he had been given a radio instead of a whistle. He stepped over to the desk, which had a microphone, and pressed a switch. Now everything he said would boom around the speakers in the Waxworld building. He cleared his throat. 'A-hem. Hello. Mr Crudge? A-hem. If you are there, can you come to your office? I have an important question to ask you. A-hem.'

He stepped out of the office and along the track of the little railway. In the stillness he could hear a faint humming as the track came alive. Mr Crudge was on his way.

You blithering, blundering, brainless bungler!

Y ou will remember that Billy Crudge had been on the Waxworld train that carried visitors around the historic scenes. He had driven Nero to the Waxworld of Rome while the red-haired girl, Molly, sat in the back.

Nero had climbed out eagerly when he saw his home city and a servant waiting with his lyre. Molly had followed and as she stepped into the scene the models came to life and she was surrounded by the sounds of the streets.

Billy Crudge was much slower, so before he stepped out of the train he heard the speakers crackle and the voice of that quaint policeman say, '*A-hem. Hello. Mr Crudge? A-hem. If you are there, can you come to your office?*'

Billy felt he should have joined the girl to enter Nero's Roman world and see that it all worked. Dr Wiggott would want a report.

The policeman's voice went on, '*I have an important question to ask you. A-hem.*' He seemed to have a bad cough.

'I'd better go and see what he wants,' the caretaker decided. 'The girl will be safe enough – it's not like the crazy old Waxworld characters ... all she has to do is press a button on her infinit-G app and the models will melt. I did remember to tell her that ... didn't I?'

Billy stepped back into the train and pressed the pedal to clatter back to the Dank Alley entrance. He was halfway there when he wondered, 'I *did* tell Molly Maltby about the power of the app, didn't I? Oh, well, I'm sure Dr Wiggott said that infinit-G models can destroy each other but can't hurt a real human. She'll be fine – stop worrying.'

He worried.

The train pulled to a halt at the small platform beside his office where PC Elloe waited.

'Hello, L.O. Elloe,' Billy said with a grin. He never tired of that little joke. 'Why do we have the honour of your company today, Constable? Has a pet rat gone missing and you've been sent to search for it? Or is it something really important? Has the sergeant sent you to get him a cup of tea?'

PC Elloe sniffed. He had a feeling Billy Crudge was making fun of him, but he wasn't sure. 'There is a girl in Wildpool—'

'There are lots of girls in Wildpool,' Billy interrupted.

'There is a girl in Wildpool called Molly Maltby. She was kidnapped last month, and I have been sent to keep an eye on her.'

'Right eye or left eye?' Billy asked.

'*Both* eyes ... a-hem...'

'Bit of a cough there, Constable.'

'We want to make sure the evil Arfur Loaf doesn't return to avenge himself on the girl who made him flee Wildpool[16].'

---

16 The adventure PC Elloe is describing has been told in the book *Wiggott's Wonderful Waxworld: Terror Train*. You should read it. It's very good.

The caretaker nodded. 'An evil man.'

'I followed her to Dank Alley and saw her enter Wiggott's. I just want to make sure she is safe.'

'Safe as the *Titanic*.'

'It sank.'

'Nothing's perfect. She is tucked away in Nero's Roman scene in the Waxworld.'

'Nero? Nero? The evillest emperor that ever ruled Rome? You left brave Molly there? You blithering, blundering, brainless bungler!' Elloe bellowed.

'You don't think it's a good idea, then,' Billy Crudge muttered.

The phone in his office rang.

There's a couple of roast thrushes if you want them

W as Molly really in danger? A claw-like hand had gripped her shoulder. Let's see who it was and if she is in deadly peril. . .

In the hot Roman roadway of Waxworld Rome, Molly looked at the man who had gripped her shoulder in his bony claw. It was a tall man in a toga[17]. The toga fell in folds as deep as the folds on the old man's fierce face.

'You are a slave, girl, and never forget it,'

17 A 'toga', if you *didn't* know, is a large white sheet that rich Romans wrapped themselves in. A 'toga' if you *did* know is *still* a large white sheet rich Romans wrapped themselves in.

the old man said. 'A Celt I rescued from the Arena. If I hadn't bought you then you'd be feeding the lions next time the games come around.'

Molly was brave, and Molly was clever. Clever enough to know that sometimes it helps to have a rich person to protect you. She put on a humble face and muttered, 'Yes, master.'

'Master *Valerius* to you, and never forget that. Wait here till the races are over. Then I expect you to find me a team of chair-carriers to carry me home up the Palatine Hill.'

'I don't get to see the chariot races, then?' the girl sighed.

Master Valerius turned pale with shock. 'The circus races are for the citizens of Rome, not slaves,' he said, and his voice was sharp as a mouthful of lemon. 'Wait for me by the pie stall over there.' The old man nodded towards a wooden bench where a shrunken woman was handing out pies to people on their way into the arena.

The arena was filling fast, and the crowded streets were emptying. All along the wooden walls were stalls selling food or selling red, green, blue or white ribbons for fans to wear.

The last few people were hurrying in and the food stalls were left with scraps. Molly was hungry now and walked along the line. She had no money with her. All she could find in her pocket was her mobile phone. The screen was dark as a sulk. She turned it on. No signal.

She came across a stall with some roasted pieces of meat and vegetables on a wooden skewer. Maybe if she smiled sweetly at the woman the stallholder would give her some. 'Any left-overs?' she asked.

The woman shrugged. 'There's a couple of roast thrushes if you want them ... they're a bit burned.'

'Thrushes?'

'Fresh today ... well, yesterday ... well, last week. Here, do you want one or not?'

Molly shook her head. The idea of being a tweeter-eater made her sick. She came to a stall where roast dormice were for sale and then next to that, one with sausages sizzling over hot charcoal in a metal bucket. The sausage-seller was greasy as his food. The sweat on his brow was dripping onto the sausage skins.

Molly wasn't hungry any longer.

She saw an empty stall covered with a cloth. There were roars from inside the arena. It was cool and quiet under the cloth. The girl pulled out the phone again and tapped the screen. She wanted to chat to Boy and see how he'd got on in Loaf Tower. Still no signal. She sighed.

They'll be thrown to the wild animals tomorrow

There was a rumble of wheels on the paved road and a strange babble of animal noises. Molly looked out and saw a parade heading for the doors of the Circus Maximus.

This was what she expected to see at a circus. Animals in cages on the back of horse-drawn wagons. Then she looked closer. They trundled past and she watched sad ostriches with bound beaks, lions with liquid eyes that could have held tears, tail-lashing crocodiles that crawled on filthy floors, bedraggled bears in chains and red-eyed boars with tusks chopped short. At the end came the elephants, too large for any cart, led on ropes with their ankles chained to stop them running.

As they entered the Circus the crowds roared to see the strange beasts led around. This was the fun they wanted before the chariot-racing started.

She slid out from under the table and asked the thrush-seller, 'What are those poor animals doing here?'

Molly's face was a mask of misery and the stallholder was puzzled. 'They are an advert for the games in the Colosseum tomorrow,' she said. 'The gladiators will hunt them while the Romans cheer every death.'

'Awful people. Why did Dr Wiggott make this wicked world?'

Molly waited till the parade had finished its long walk round the Circus Maximus. The wagons rolled out of the dark doorway they had entered ten minutes before. Molly watched them driven back towards the road.

One wagon waited outside for the parade to finish. The cage on the back was filled with skinny people in rags. Some carried crosses made of wood or straw. Some were too weary and weak to hold up a feather.

'Celts and Christians,' the thrush-seller explained. 'They'll be thrown to the wild animals tomorrow.'

'Can't we save them?' Molly cried.

The woman shook her head. 'Why would you want to? It's not as if they are Roman citizens.'

Molly muttered to herself, 'But if they decide I'm a Celt ... if I am thrown to the lions tomorrow ... will I survive? Is this infinit-G world really as safe as Mr Crudge says?'

Molly frowned. 'Visitors to Wiggott's Wonderful Waxworld stepped off the train and were never seen again[18]. Maybe this really is dangerous. I think I need to find Dr Wiggott as soon as possible then get out as fast as I can. If I don't, I may never escape.'

She needed help. It was on its way ... well, a hopeless sort of help, but stranger things have happened.

---

18 That was in the old Waxworld, Molly. Are you saying you don't trust the amazing Dr Wiggott? No? You may be right.

Half the windows in Wildpool were blown out

The Ladies Who Crunch had met again at the Top Coffee Café with fresh coffees. They looked grim as Grimsby and twice as ugly. Marjorie Doors took out her knitting and clacked away faster than her chattering false teeth on a winter's day.

'Lady Frankenstone's infinit-G chip has been stolen by Boy. Does that mean she can't make any more monsters? She destroyed the others in the Town Hall. We saw them melt.'

'She can't make more at the moment. There are only two infinit-G chips in the world – Dr Wiggott has one. Boy has the other,' Minnie Cooper said happily.

She looked into her coffee cup. The coffee had tiny ripples on top, as if someone were shaking the café.

'No monsters means no horrors attraction at Frankenstone Castle,' Marjorie said.

'She still has Frankenstone's monster. Boy said he saw it in Loaf Tower – the monster with its skull stitched together and a bolt through its neck[19],' Edna Crudge said. She was thinking hard.

The ripples on the coffees grew bigger. The table began to tremble and the cups to rattle in their saucers.

'It's an earthquake,' Minnie gasped. 'I haven't seen one of them since 1946.'

Edna snapped at her, 'There's never been an earthquake in Wildpool, Minnie. You have more wool between your ears than Marjorie has in her knitting box.'

Minnie narrowed her eyes. 'You can be very cruel, Edna. If your tongue gets any sharper,

---

19 A top tip here. If your head ever falls off, fasten it back on with a bolt. I went to school with a girl who did that. We called her the Head Girl. (Or I could be lying.)

you'll cut your tonsils. In the last war there were bombs that fell on Wildpool. One fell in the canal but didn't explode. Then, one day in 1946, it went off. Half the windows in Wildpool were blown out and some old buildings were shaken to the ground. But not my lovely cottage in Pump Street. Built to last, they are.'

'Sorry, Minnie, I apologise. But that doesn't feel like a bomb to me.'

'No,' Marjorie said, looking out of the window. 'It'll be that giant crane rolling down the street.'

The Ladies Who Crunch looked out. Marjorie was right. A towering web of iron on caterpillar tracks was edging its way past Loaf Tower. Igon, the man in the eyepatch, was waving to the driver to guide it around a corner.

'What's that big ball on a chain at the top?' Minnie asked.

'It's a wrecking ball, Minnie,' Edna said quietly.

'And where's it heading...?' she began to ask, then swallowed hard. 'It's going to Pump Street, isn't it? It's going to knock my cottage down.' A tear glittered in the corner of one eye.

Minnie wiped it away and blew her nose. 'And I can't do anything to stop it.'

'Oh, but I can,' Edna said. She picked up her smartphone and found the number she wanted. It rang for a while until Billy Crudge answered it. 'Billy? I have a job for you. Listen very carefully. We don't have much time.'

You pour the gloop into the tray on the bench

While Edna worried about Minnie's cottage on Pump Street, no one was worried about Molly Maltby . . . no one except Constable L.O. Elloe. Remember that outburst? "'You left brave Molly there? You blithering, blundering, brainless bungler!' Elloe bellowed[20]"?

'You don't think it's a good idea then,' Billy Crudge muttered. And that was the moment when the phone in his office rang.

'I'd better get that,' the caretaker said, glad to get away from the angry policeman

---

20 I can only apologise for PC Elloe's strong language. I wasn't expecting that sort of passion from such a shy man. Sorry. It may happen again.

whose face had turned red with rage – red as Lady Frankenstone's fingernails (after they'd been freshly painted). He slid away into his office and picked up the phone.

You may think it was his wife, Edna, ringing to ask him to help save Minnie's cottage. And *if* you thought that then you'd be *right*. How did you know? How did you ever get to be so clever? What? You read the end of the last chapter? Fair enough.

You could say they chatted on the phone but a 'chat' usually has *two* people taking part. Edna wasn't in a 'chatty' mood; she was in a 'bossy' mood. She gave the orders, and Billy grunted his replies.

'Billy? I have a job for you. Listen very carefully. We don't have much time,' Edna said.

'PC Elloe—'

'You have helped Dr Wiggott turn a bucket of gloop into a character.'

'Err...'

'You pour the gloop into the tray on the bench, then you go to the computer.'

'Yes.'

'And you put in the name of the character you want to create ... then you wait while the computer researches the name.'

'PC Elloe says—'

'Shut up and listen. The computer screen will say something like, "About 18,900 results in 0.68 seconds. If you are sure you've got the right character, go to the bench."'

'Got that—'

'Make sure the infinit-G chip is in the slot...'

'Obviously.'

'And press GO. Stand back and watch the character take shape. You've seen it done by Dr Wiggott.'

'Fifty times,' Billy agreed. 'We made all the characters that are in Nero's Roman world.'

'Good. Here's the name of the character I want you to create. When he's ready, bring him to the Top Coffee Café. Do you have a pen? You never were very good at spelling. Boy is on his way to Dank Lane now with the second infinit-G. He'll help.'

And Billy wrote down the name. 'Talking about Nero's Roman world, I took Nero along to finish the scene off, and Molly went with me.' He stopped. There was a buzzing in his ear. A dial tone. Edna had hung up. She was gone.

He looked out of the office window to the platform. The little train was gone. And so was PC Elloe.

I've never met a sausage thief

Molly sat in the gloom under the Roman bread-seller's table to wait for Master Valerius to come out. In the warm Roman air, she began to doze. She slept for maybe ten minutes then woke with a start.

The roars from the Circus Maximus came and went like waves on a seashore. But that wasn't what had woken her. She listened. There it was. The sound of a metal stud on the sole of a sandal scraping on a stone in the road.

Molly had learned a lot from her friend Boy, who knew all about footsteps. She now knew about footsteps that were running away, and footsteps that were creeping up. And these were creeping-up-type footsteps.

She slowly raised a corner of the cloth on the table and looked out. She smiled. She knew she was right. The sandals were on the feet of a man, and the man was trying to tiptoe. If the girl pushed her head out she would be able to see the man's face. If she could see the man's face, then the man could see her too.

The sun on the stone street dazzled Molly for a while but she watched the feet walk towards her. On the next stall she heard the sausage pan being lifted off the table.

'A sausage thief? I've never met a sausage thief,' she giggled.

The footsteps walked behind the table. But Molly knew there was nothing behind the table except the wooden wall of the Circus Maximus. She risked looking out. She saw the legs of the man and watched the thief take the pan and throw the contents towards the wood wall.

Fat splattered; sausages dropped to the dust. The man threw the pan on the ground and came back to the sausage table. This time he seemed to be struggling as he lifted the cloth off the table. If the man looked round now he'd see the young spy.

Molly held her breath. The man wasn't interested in what was under the table. He was picking up the pan full of glowing charcoal. He was using the cloth to hold the handle, so his hands wouldn't burn and turn his fingers into ten charred sausages[21].

He shuffled across to the fat-splattered wall. Molly had been holding her breath so long she felt she'd burst. She let out the breath in a gasp as the man threw the hot charcoal at the fatty wooden wall. 'No,' Molly breathed.

The charcoal glowed. When it met the greasy wood, it flickered into a flame. The flame spread quickly upwards to become a blaze. The flames sucked in air to help them burn and Molly felt the draught *shush* past her.

The sandals were running away now. Molly jumped out from under the table and watched the man in a dirty tunic running. When the

---

21 Fried fingers are really quite tasty. When I was a kid my mum fed me them every night for tea. 'Here you are, son, your favourites,' she would say. 'Fried fish fingers.'

fire-maker reached the corner, he turned to make sure his fire was well under way. At that moment his eyes met Molly's. Eyes as mad as a box of frogs. Eyes that Molly has seen in Dr Wiggott's workshop and on the train, sitting next to Mr Crudge.

'Nero?' she gasped. 'Nero.'

She'll grow to be a rebel
and then you'll be sorry

Emperor Nero's face was a fury of fierceness as fiery as the flames he'd just lit. He looked murderous. His hand flew to the short sword at his belt. He took a step towards Molly Maltby. The girl did not have a sword . . . but she did have a throat that would slice very nicely if Nero caught her.

Molly raced for the entrance to the Circus Maximus[22]. She let the darkness of the entrance passages swallow her and hide her.

Inside, Master Valerius was enjoying the

---

22 'Is she *mad*?' you cry. 'No one with any sense runs *into* a burning building. You wouldn't run into a burning building. Or maybe you would, if the choice was either that or facing nutty Nero with a nasty knife. (But please don't.) [?]

races. He knew Emperor Nero's greens would win because the emperor hated losing. Emperor Nero would make *sure* they won. He bribed rival riders, or arranged for the other teams' wheels to wobble, or for their horses to be fed with too much hay and water. He had to cheat to beat the reds, whites and blues.

Valerius was a green. Of course. The crowd went quiet in the wait between races.

'I nearly missed the first race,' Valerius said to the bald man with mighty muscles on his left. 'The streets were so crowded. My slave was dragging her feet. Looking at all the sights. She's never been to Rome before.'

The muscled man gave a muscled chuckle. 'You don't have a good whip to beat her with?'

'A beating could kill her, she's such a frail thing,' Valerius argued.

'Take my advice, friend. Beat her every day or she'll be spoilt. She'll grow to be a rebel and then you'll be sorry.'

'I'll buy a whip on the way home ... friend,' Valerius said, and nodded.

'Ah, here are the horses now,' his new friend said.

There was a red ribbon round his wrist. 'Who are you supporting?'

'Erm... Red, of course... Who else?' Valerius lied.

The one-horse chariots were coloured red or blue or green or white and lined up at the starting gate with riders snarling challenges at one another. The crowd cat-called the opposition and cheered their favourites as they were announced.

The starter bellowed, 'For the blues we have Quintus Flavius, champion at Pompeii last week. For the reds it is a newcomer, Julius Agricola. The whites have the Thracian slave Optimus Brutus and of course the emperor's green team have Marcus Imperatus.' There was loud booing for the emperor's rider. To the charioteers the starter said, 'Are you ready? Back, Green, back to the mark or you will be disqualified.'

As Green reversed the starter dropped a flag and the horses dashed off, leaving Green a length behind. The crowd jeered.

Lost in the sound of the cheers was the voice of a girl. 'Fire! Get out! Fire!'

But let's leave Molly to scream. We need to see what Edna has done to save Minnie's cottage. . .

Keep your help and stick it under your eyepatch, pal

'Left hand down a bit,' Igon shouted to the driver of the crane with the wrecking ball. Igon was a small man. The driver was even smaller – Igon had a thin, pale face under his hairy head; the driver had a beetroot face under hair like exploding dandelion seeds.

'You'll put your crane through the butcher's shop window if you're not careful,' Igon groaned.

The crane had been running along far faster than a frightened tortoise being chased by a snail. The red-face driver stopped and opened the window of his cab. When he spoke, it was with the gentle voice of a Scotsman who had gargled with broken glass. 'Don't you tell me how to drive my crane. I've been driving this beauty for forty years and I've hardly ever hit a window ... not more than one a month in all that time.'

'That's an awful lot of windows,' the butcher said, coming out of his shop with a meat axe swinging by his side. 'Just be careful, pal.'

'Don't call me "pal" ... my name is James. Show a craftsman some respect, or else.'

'Or else what?' the butcher growled. He was a large man with greasy hair and bad teeth.

'Or else I will raise the jib of this crane and swing the wrecking ball at your shop. It'll be more than a window that gets breaked. Three swings of this bad boy and your scruffy little shop will be broken bricks and dust.'

The Ladies Who Crunch were sitting at a table outside the Top Coffee Café, enjoying the argument. Edna said, 'The longer they argue, the more time Billy has to put my plan into action.'

'You make the best plans in Wildpool, Edna,' Minnie said. 'But you haven't told us what this one *is*.'

'With any luck, you'll see,' she said grimly. 'I only hope Boy gets here in time.'

Driver James jumped to the ground. The butcher stepped forward. The top of James's head reached the belt of the butcher's blood-smeared white coat. 'I'd like to see you try,' Butcher Brown snarled.

'I'd like to see you stop me,' Driver James snarled back.

Igon stepped between them, 'Gentlemen, gentlemen, there is no need for this. Let me guide James around this corner and then it's full steam ahead to Pump Street.'

'My beauty runs on diesel, not steam,' James said.

'In that case it's ... erm ... full diesel ahead to Pump Street. Back in your cab, James. Can I give you a hand up?'

The driver's face turned from red to purple. 'Are you saying I'm too short to climb up into my own cab, you one-eyed weirdy? Is that what you're saying? Well, is it? Eh?'

'No, no, no. I was just trying to help,' Igon babbled.

'You can keep your help and stick it under your eyepatch, pal.' There was a short set of iron rungs on the side of the crane and the driver swung himself up like a long-armed ape. He started the engine and reached for the lever that would put it into gear. Then he stopped. He stared.

The butcher turned around to see what the driver was looking at. He stared. A crowd had gathered to see the fight[23]. *They* stared.

A man stood there. His long hair was the colour of autumn leaves. It flowed out of his wide-brimmed hat and over the white collar of his quaint old suit. 'Good day, good people. I'm looking for King James,' he said, and his voice sounded like a man from the North.

Driver James stuck his head out of the cab. 'I'm James King. What do you want with me?'

The man in the hat smiled through his thick moustaches then raised his hat politely. 'I've come to blow you up, your Majesty.'

'Blow me up!' James King screeched and sweat

23 Have you noticed how people do that? They do it from the early days in the school playground to their later days in their care homes. They all want to see a fight. Oh, they don't want to *be* in a fight and get a punch on the nose. But they want to see someone else's blood on the floor. Nero's Romans were just the same. People haven't changed in two thousand years. Aren't folk funny?

poured out from his forehead. 'Why? I don't even know you.'

'Then allow me to introduce myself,' the man said and swept his hat wide as he bowed. 'My name is Fawkes. Guy Fawkes.'

I saved your life, you old fool

I n Nero's Waxworld Rome, the horses raced down to the turning post at the western end with flailing whips and clashing wheels. Red got there first but Blue side-swiped them and Red crashed into the barrier. The chariot was splintered, and the rider thrown to the sandy arena where he rolled and dodged the flying hooves[24].

The crowd gave an immense roar. It drowned out Molly's pleading, 'The Circus is on fire.'

Valerius looked at the red wreckage and chuckled, 'Serves him right.'

---

24 If you saw this you'd wail, 'Oh, what a terrible accident!' But the Romans thought this was the greatest fun they could have ... apart from eating a thrush or watching Christians being eaten by lions.

His red-ribboned friend said, 'You what?'

Valerius swallowed hard and remembered which team the large man supported. 'I said … what a sight.'

The bald man glared. 'You sure you're not one of Emperor Nero's supporters, are you?'

'Me? Nero? No. Dreadful man. I'm Valerius from outside the Praetorian Gate. We can't stand nutty Nero out there.'

'Not many people can,' the red fan said. They shared a laugh.

Molly suddenly saw Master Valerius in the crowd. 'Run for your life, Master! The Circus is on fire!'

Valerius turned angrily, not wishing to miss a moment of the race. Then he saw smoke billowing over the outer walls of the circus. People started to cry out. Everyone rose to their feet and headed for the exits in a tangle of togas and tunics. A Roman soldier took charge.

'Open the main gates,' he ordered as people surged past him.

Large gates in the Circus walls burst open and the crowd tumbled out. The fire was spreading, and the crowd burst into a fire-flight. Valerius stood near an exit and looked around him. Molly struggled to stay on her feet as she ran out. Valerius snatched at her shoulder.

'You were told to wait outside.'

'I saved your life, you old fool,' Molly exploded.

'Old fool? Old fool? I am *not* old... It's a whip for you, slave-girl,' he shouted and dragged the girl into the street. 'That Red fan was right ... a whip will cure your cheeky tongue.'

Choking smoke began to fill the street, as everyone ran. The Circus Maximus burned angrily, and large sparks started to crackle and fly over the city. A weathervane spun and strained in the wind.

'Why is no one trying to put out the fire?' Molly asked. No one listened.

Sparks from the bright fire of the Circus had begun to spread, further and further across the city. The Romans weren't running from the flames. They were running to save their homes.

Many of them would be too late.

Next time Nero sees you he'll have you killed

Master Valerius dragged Molly through the streets and up one of the steep hills out of Rome. 'The wind is from the west. The city may burn, but my house is safe,' he said.

'Shouldn't we help the poor people put out the fires?' the girl asked. She looked back to see Rome become a bonfire. Whirling sparks from the Circus landed on roofs of houses. People scrambled to beat out the flames or ran for jars of water. But as they beat out one flame another sprang up. The water sizzled and spat and turned to steam.

Master Valerius pushed Molly along the stone-paved path, past gleaming marble pillars towards his fine villa on the hilltop. She would not be allowed inside the polished oak doors. Valerius set her to work in the stables where fine horses were fed and groomed better than the slaves that cared for them. Looking after the fine animals was a task that every slave wanted. It wasn't Molly's task. Her job was to clean out the donkey's stall, feed it and water it. The donkey kicked and bit and Molly had to dodge as she worked.

The sun began to set but the flames of Rome burned bright as the sun. A shy slave-girl brought Molly some cheese for supper. She said her name was Livia. Together they chewed on cheese in their bedroom ... the hayloft over the donkey's stable. Molly told her tale of seeing Nero start the great fire.

'Better keep that quiet,' Livia whispered. 'The servants are saying that Nero is sending out soldiers to look for a girl with Celt-red hair. It won't end happily if they find her.'

'How do I get back to Dr Wiggott's Waxworld?' Molly groaned.

'Who is Wiglet?' the slave asked.

'A very powerful person who can be very stupid.'

'A bit like our Emperor Nero,' the slave sighed. 'He's crazy and cruel. How do you think he became emperor?'

Molly shrugged wearily. Mucking out donkeys is hard work for a girl whose fingers are used to pushing pens and clattering keyboards. She didn't want a history test. 'I don't know how Nero became emperor. I suppose his dad was emperor and he died.'

'His *step*-father was Emperor Claudius. He was poisoned with mushrooms . . . and some Romans say Nero did it. He poisoned his step-brother, Britannicus, too[25].'

Molly yawned. 'Thanks, Livia. I won't eat his mushrooms if he offers me any.'

'He tried to kill his own mother in a shipwreck. . .'

'I won't go sailing with him,' Molly promised. Her eyes were heavy now.

'You have to escape,' Livia cried.

25 You don't want to *know* what he did to his old teacher. You do? Oh, well, Nero ordered his teacher to kill himself – if the teacher didn't, Nero would have him executed. *You* wouldn't treat your old teacher like that, would you? (Better not answer that.)

'In the morning,' Molly said. 'Nero may poison princes, but he won't bother me.'

'Idiot,' Livia snapped. 'You saw him start the fire. If he sees you again he'll want to shut you up. Next time Nero sees you he'll have you killed. Understand?'

But Molly was snoring. She needed help. And help was on its way.

Big bad burglars don't bother me, hah

PC Laurence Olivier Elloe was shocked when he heard that Molly Maltby had entered the twisted trail of rails that ran around Wiggott's Wonderful Waxworld. 'The sergeant told me to look after her. I don't care what old Mr Crudge says about her being safe. I need to check.'

The caretaker was talking to his wife on the office telephone and seemed to be taking for ever. Elloe shuffled from foot to foot and looked down at the boots that were doing the shuffling. 'They'll sack me. They'll take my lovely boots away. And my favourite truncheon ... even though I do have the biggest collection of truncheons in the whole of Wildpool,' he said, proudly patting the ebony baton on his belt.

He checked his equipment. He had done it before he left the house. He had done it when he arrived at the police station to report for duty. He had done it when he was marching up and down Dank Alley. 'You can never check too many times. A thief could steal something when I wasn't looking,' he sighed. 'There are a lot of thieves around. Someone should arrest them.'

The handcuffs were clipped to his belt. His police radio was there and the can of spray that would sting the eyes of any ruthless rebel rioter or big bad burglar. 'Big bad burglars don't bother me, hah,' he said. 'What is Mr Crudge *doing* all this time?' he groaned. 'My police notebook – very important ... and my pens ... one blue and one red. One torch and ooooh...'

He looked down at his belt and saw his X26 Taser – an electric shock gun that fired two darts at a cunning criminal and brought them to their knees. Now, PC L.O. Elloe wasn't afraid of ruthless rebel rioters or big bad burglars ...

but he was terrified by his Taser gun. 'What if it went off by accident and I shot myself in the foot[26]?'

PC Elloe decided the best way to overcome his Taser terror was to forget it was there. So, when he checked his equipment he patted his X26 and said, 'Taser? Not there.'

Now he said, 'Molly? Not here. I must find her. I must boldly go into Wiggott's Wonderful Waxworld and boldly take the little bold train to Nero's Roman world. And I must do it boldly.'

He stepped into the cab of the train, pressed the pedal on the floor and rattled off into the dim blue light. When Billy Crudge finished his phone call he looked for PC Elloe and – just like the constable's X26 Taser – there he wasn't.

The policeman rattled and clattered past body-snatchers and pirates, Viking warriors and hideous highwaymen. When he reached the Roman scene, he took his foot off the pedal and the train creaked to a halt. He took a deep breath and stepped into the scene.

Smoke stung his nostrils and Romans rushed

---

26 You have to agree, putting fifty thousand volts of electricity through your foot is a shocking thought. You might even call it a stocking thought.

around with leather buckets and blankets to beat out flames. He stopped an old woman who was looking at the ruin of her sausage stall. 'Excuse me,' he said politely. 'I'm looking for a girl with red pigtails.'

'The Celt traitor? We're all looking for her. Nero says she started the fire and there's a reward for anyone who can capture her, dead or alive.'

'Oh dear,' PC Elloe muttered. 'I'd better find her first, then.'

But I love
my crane too

'My name is Fawkes. Guy Fawkes.' The Wildpool crowd gasped. You would gasp.

A little girl, out shopping with her mother, said, 'Mummy. Mummy? How can that be Guy Fawkes? We burned him on a bonfire last November.'

'A dummy.'

'No, thank you, I'm too old for a dummy, Mummy.'

Her mother rolled her eyes. 'You get your beauty from your mother, Araminta. It's a shame you get your brains from your father. Now let's see what Mr Fawkes has to say.'

And Mr Fawkes spoke. 'I have a bomb here, King James,' he said to the crane driver. He held a metal ball in his hand. It was about the size of a balloon and it had a fuse sticking out from the top. 'In my pocket I have a tinder-box. Once the fuse is lit it will take two minutes before the bomb explodes. Time enough for everyone to get to safety.'

'So, you aren't planning to blow me up?' the crane driver James King said in a voice that quaked.

'No, no, no, your Majesty. I tried that back in 1605 and it didn't work. Nay, lad, I just plan to put the bomb under your vehicle,' Guy Fawkes explained.

James King's mouth fell open. 'My precious crane. I built it forty years ago; I fastened every nut and bolt myself.' A tear began to fill his eye. 'I call her Jane, after my wife.'

Igon stepped forward and handed him a clean handkerchief to wipe away the tears. 'Don't you ever get them mixed up?' he asked.

'Well, laddie, Jane the Wife's a woman, and Jane the Crane's a fifty-tonne bit of metal with a wrecking ball on the end. But, yes, I do mix them up from time to time.'

Guy Fawkes was kneeling beside his bomb and striking a flint on a piece of rough metal till sparks flew and the fuse caught alight. 'You won't have that problem any more. I'm going to blow Jane to pieces.'

'No-o-o,' James King moaned. 'I love my wife.'

Araminta sighed. 'I think Mr Fawkes means he's going to blow up Jane the Crane, not your wife.'

'Sorry,' the crane driver muttered. 'But I love my crane too.'

'And Minnie Cooper loves her cottage in Pump Street,' Marjorie Doors shouted from the Top Coffee Café where the Ladies Who Crunch had been watching the argument.

'You have two minutes to get a hundred metres away from the bomb,' Guy cried. The fuse fizzed and sparked.

'Was this part of your plan, Edna?' Minnie asked. 'If that crane topples it'll wreck our café.'

'I thought Guy would blow it up further down the street outside the Town Hall,' Edna sighed.

'I had a back-up plan, but it's too late now. We'd better make a run for it.'

As the Ladies Who Crunch began to hobble and shuffle down the street[27], they heard a scream that rattled the weathervane on the Town Hall tower. A mother screamed one word. 'Araminta!'

27 Would they get far enough? Probably not. Ladies Who Crunch, crunched.

Everything, I've thought of everything

The crowd had been running from the bomb in a panic. They stopped, turned and stared. The little girl with pink ribbons in her hair, pink bows on her shoes and pink socks in her pink shoes was walking the other way. She was walking towards the fizzing fuse.

'Araminta, run!' her mother cried.

'Run, Araminta!' the crowd cried[28].

The girl looked under the crane where Guy Fawkes had left the bomb.

'Come here at once, Minty,' her mother said.

---

28 All except one old man who said, 'Araminta? What sort of name is that to give a child, eh?' But the old man's name was Derek, so he had no right to complain.

'If you don't come here I will take your tablet from you and you won't play Pony Club Crush ever again.'

Araminta shrugged. 'I've seen this on one of my computer games. The fuse burns down till it reaches the gunpowder inside. Then it explodes. All you have to do is pull the fuse out.' She began to crawl under the tracks.

A-ra-*min*-ta,' her mother raged. 'That's your best dress. You'll ruin it crawling down a dirty street. Get up at once or you'll never have fish fingers again.'

The little girl ignored her, reached out and dragged the bomb out from under the crane. 'One minute,' Guy Fawkes shouted from the safety of a passageway as dark as Dank Alley.

She wrapped her tiny hand around the thick cord that made the fuse and pulled. The cord stayed stuck in the metal case. Guy Fawkes peered out from his hiding place. 'I thought of that. I glued it in. I'm not stupid, you know.'

'You were stupid enough to get caught four hundred years ago,' the little girl snapped.

'Thirty seconds,' Fawkes shouted.

'Run, Araminta, run!' the crowd shouted as she sat on the road and stared at the sparkling fuse as if it were a computer-game problem.

There were two centimetres of fuse left to burn and it looked like there would soon be pink ribbons flying from the Town Hall weathervane.

A shadow appeared over the girl's shoulder. It was Minnie Cooper with a cup of coffee. Araminta looked cross. 'Elderly lady, you really should be a long way away.'

'Ten seconds,' Guy Fawkes shouted.

The crowd began to count, every number louder than the one before.

'Nine … eight … seven … six…'

'Everything, I've thought of everything,' Guy Fawkes cried.

'Three … two…'

Minnie poured her cup of coffee over the fuse and it spluttered out.

'I never thought of that,' Guy Fawkes sighed.

'Elderly lady, you have saved the crane and lost your house,' Araminta said.

Minnie grinned. 'Maybe. Maybe not. Edna has a plan … a back-up plan … and Edna Crudge never lets a friend down. Now run along back to your mum. And, Araminta. . .'

'Yes, elderly lady?'

'I hope you grow up to have a friend like Edna.'

No, no. I can't let Nero see me

Molly woke. She felt fresh. She'd slept in worse places than a soft hayloft. She grinned at the slave-girl Livia. 'Good morning, Livia. Do you know your way around Rome?'

'Of course,' the girl said, and she scowled.

'Time to get back to the Waxworld train. I came into Nero's Roman world near the chariot arena. Can you show me the way back?'

'Go to the gate and I'll point the way,' Livia offered. 'I don't want to be seen with you when Nero's guards capture you.'

'Makes sense.' Molly nodded. 'I don't want to

get you punished for being a friend. But it's early. There won't be many guards around at this time.'

Livia held out a scarf. It was grubby, grey wool. 'Put that over your head ... it's the hair that will give you away.'

Molly smiled. 'Thanks, Livia. When I get back I'll make sure Dr Wiggott gives you a better life in here.'

Livia just stared blankly at her. 'Mad.'

'Not as mad as Nero,' Molly said.

The dawn sky was just growing a lemon-yellow and marigold-orange light. Molly lowered herself from the loft and walked towards the barn door.

'Left at the front gate and down the hill...' Livia began.

But Molly's path was blocked by Master Valerius. 'Ah, there you are, girl. Is my donkey saddled?' he fussed. 'It was the last thing I told you to do. I said, "Have the donkey saddled to take me into the city this morning." Is it ready?'

Molly shook her head. 'Do it,' Livia whispered. 'The donkey will get you safely into the city and then you can look for your way out.'

Molly ran to the donkey and threw a blanket

and leather pad over the evil-eyed creature. As she tightened the strap under the saddle the donkey turned its head and nipped her back. Molly jumped and cried out.

'Hurry,' Master Valerius nagged. 'The great men of Rome meet in the Senate[29] and I need to be there.'

Molly led the donkey out and helped the Roman onto its back. It refused to move. Valerius gave it a slap with a whip he was carrying, and it set off so quickly Molly had to jog to keep up. It seemed that Valerius could make the animal move but not steer it. 'Take the reins, girl,' he ordered.

The yellow sky was stained with mud-brown clouds of throat-gagging smoke. The city below them was a patchwork of blackened buildings that smouldered and some that still glowed cinder red. Molly trotted ahead, holding the leading rein of the donkey, while Master Valerius snapped out his orders. 'Left here and then the Senate is straight ahead. We need to get there before Emperor Nero.'

---

29 The place in Rome where posh men met to talk. Sadly, women had no say. That could be why the Roman Empire is gone. They should have made it a No-man Empire.

Molly stumbled as her knees went weak. 'Nero? No, no. I can't let Nero see me.'

'Nero is not interested in some scrawny slave. He is a god. He sees only the great lords of Rome.'

'Maybe he needs his eyes tested?' Molly muttered. 'I hope you're right, Master ... and he doesn't see me.'

I'll slice you into pieces and throw the bits into the River Tiber

The great fire hadn't touched the Senate.
The fine building stood solid but smoke-
stained, with its great marble pillars and floors
undamaged. Lordly men in togas stood outside.
Shabby servants held their horses and carriages,
donkeys and chairs. Some of the great men
were young and some even older than Valerius.
They all looked angry.

Guards with scarred and teak-hard faces

blocked the way. 'The Praetorian Guard,' Valerius said. 'The emperor's own little army of loyal men. He must be worried.'

'Nero? Worried?'

'Yes. The word is going around Rome that Nero ordered someone to start the fire,' Valerius said quietly.

'But he did,' Molly said.

'What was that?' Valerius asked.

'But ... he ... did ... want the city cleared to make room for his palace,' the girl said louder.

Valerius grunted. 'Don't say that too loud or you'll be thrown off the Tarpeian Rock. The fate of traitors who upset the emperor.'

'Would it kill me?' Molly asked.

'Of course ... unless you can bounce,' Valerius said and gave a cruel grin. 'That was a joke, girl. You may laugh.'

'Haa,' Molly said weakly.

'Now help me down. This is the place where the great men of Rome meet. Men like me. The emperor will come here to answer some tough questions. You see? The guards are letting the great and the good of Rome inside.'

Molly helped Master Valerius down from the donkey and Valerius marched into the Senate alongside a man with a wig of golden hair. 'Nero has gone too far this time,' they agreed, but they spoke quietly with looks over their shoulders.

Suddenly a man jumped up on to a fountain edge. 'It's all Nero's fault,' he cried. Two guards quickly ran over and pulled him off and dragged him away screaming. The crowd of people fall silent. The Praetorian Guardsmen looked menacing. They were stopping the senators and searching them for weapons.

Valerius strode past a guard. 'I am Valerius. Senior council member of the Praetorian District.'

'Good for you,' the guard sneered. He gave a disrespectful nod of the head to show the old man could pass inside the Senate. Molly watched him go.

'Now's the time to flee,' she decided. She found the donkey and climbed onto its back. She kicked it. The donkey didn't move.

She slapped it. The donkey didn't move.

Molly jumped to the ground. 'Just have to run

for it,' she sighed. She turned. She came face to brass with a guard's breastplate.

'You can't leave that donkey there, slave. Either take it away or stay with it till your master comes out ... or else I'll slice you into pieces and throw the bits into the River Tiber[30],' the scar-cheeked soldier said. 'Now stand back. Here comes Emperor Nero.'

---

30 Nonsense. The guard was bluffing. Quick history lesson here: Nero didn't have his enemies cut up and thrown into the river Tiber. People had to *drink* that water. No, Nero had them cut up and thrown into the city sewers. *Much* cleaner.

Do you want a punch up the hooter?

M olly pulled the grey scarf tightly over her head. The emperor looked different now. Molly had seen him dressed as a race-fan in a grubby tunic when had started the fire. Now the emperor was in a snow-white toga with purple edges. He wore a glittering crown of gold.

Molly had seen the fire-maker snarling and waving a knife. This man was smiling and waving to the curious crowds outside the Senate. But Molly knew those cruel eyes that dazzled brighter than the gold crown. This was the same man. The man who threw sausage fat at the

Circus Maximus and turned the silver marbled city black. 'No. He's a model made by Wiggott,' she tried to tell herself.

'Oi, slave,' a voice called. Molly looked up. Nero's chariot driver was looming over her, leaning out of a one-horse chariot pulled by a fine black stallion.

'Yes?'

'You're a groom-slave. . .'

'Not exactly. . .'

'So, hold on to the emperor's horse while I go for a breakfast sausage.'

'It's a powerful horse. Do you think I can hold it?'

'Of course. It's well trained by my own fair hand. And fast as the wind.' The charioteer was leaned closer to the girl and whispered, 'In case we need to make a fast getaway, know what I mean? There's a piece of silver in it for you, lass.'

The man patted Molly on the head and hurried off against the tide of the crowd who were following Nero into the Senate where they could hear the speeches inside. Even the mighty Praetorian Guard couldn't stem the flow.

Molly tied the black stallion to the donkey – it was the most solid thing in the square. She looked at the scar-cheeked soldier. 'Would you look after the horse and donkey for me? There's a piece of silver in it for you.'

The soldier's eyes glinted with greed. 'I'm not going anywhere,' he said. 'May as well.'

Molly joined the crowd heading to the doorway. She stayed in the shadows and slipped into a corner by a statue. The great men were talking a lot and making a great deal of noise. The words 'Nero', 'fire' and 'palace' could be heard. 'What am I doing?' Molly cried. 'I need to be escaping[31].' She pulled out her smartphone, hoping to find a map of Nero's Rome. There was no signal. 'You're no help,' she muttered at the phone. But help *was* on the way.

No. That's not quite true. There was someone on their way to help her. But that someone may not be much help when they got there because

---

31 She didn't reply. How rude is that? If someone asks you a question you should always be polite and reply ... even if the person asking the question is yourself. Good manners cost nothing. Be told.

they had a brain like a bowl of porridge. A bowl of porridge without a spoon. And this bold rescuer's name? You can guess...

I may not have a later date, mate

P C Elloe had wandered the streets of Rome
looking for a red-haired girl with pigtails
and now he saw a crowd of grim-faced people
crossing a wide square in the middle of the city.
'Where is everyone going?' he asked a beggar on
a street corner. The man had a white cloth round
his eyes as if he was blind.

'They'll be off to the Senate,' the beggar
said with a nod. 'Have you got a bit of spare
change?'

PC Elloe glared at him. 'I should arrest you.
Begging is illegal under the Vagrancy Act of 1824.

It does not carry a jail sentence, although the Act applies in all public places.'

'I am not begging. I am selling maps of Rome for visitors. I am what you might call a tour guide ... not a beggar.'

PC Elloe reached down and picked up a map, drawn in ink on a dirty piece of paper. 'I'll take this.'

'One denarius,' the beggar said.

'As an officer of the law I am commandeering this,' the policeman said.

'Commandeering? What's *commandeering* mean?' the beggar asked.

'It means I am taking it without payment. You may apply to Wildpool Police Station for payment at a later date.'

'A later date? A later *date*? I may not have a later date, mate. I may have died of hunger. You can't steal my map—'

'Commandeer.'

'All right... You can't common-tea the map of a poor beggar,' the beggar wailed.

'I thought you said you weren't a beggar,' PC Elloe said, quick as a slug with athlete's foot.

The beggar raised the eye-cloth and glared at the constable. 'I *wasn't* a beggar till some evil law officer stole my map. I couldn't go on with my career as a *tour guide* without my map, could I? You drove me to begging.'

'I'll drive you to the courts in a police van,' PC Elloe threatened.

'Do you want a punch up the hooter[32]?' the beggar asked, throwing off his eye bandage and starting to get to his feet.

'Threatening a police officer *will* land you in jail. Lucky for you I am busy searching for a red-haired girl.'

'Huh,' the beggar snorted. 'We *all* are... Finding the red-haired girl would be like winning Nero's lottery. She has no chance. Like the Green fans sing, "Red-red-red, soon be dead."'

'Not if I can help it,' a grim PC Elloe said. Grimly.

---

32 How offensive is that? A polite person, like you, would say, politely, 'Would you like a punch up the bracket?'

The ugliest, thugliest men and women of Blackbird Hill

When the Wildpool bomb scare was over, Araminta ran back to her mother, whose face was as pink as her daughter's dress. The child was dragged home to change out of her road-stained clothes. The crowd clapped for the brave child then started to drift away.

Nobody had died. 'I am so pleased nobody died,' the woman with a shopping bag sighed. But in truth she sounded a little disappointed. Like the crowds in Nero's Rome, they came to see someone suffer … so long as it wasn't them. Rome… Wildpool? Different places, different times – same people.

Nero… Lady Frankenstone? Different people, different clothes – same evil.

Igon sniggered and wiped a tear from his eye and a tear from the eyepatch. 'Oh dear, Guy Fawkes. A loser in 1605 and a loser now in Wildpool.'

The gunpowder plotter stepped out from the passage where he'd been hiding. His teeth shone white under the autumn-brown moustaches. 'Oh dear, Igon. A loser when Boy defeated you once before, and a loser now.'

Igon looked cross. 'Loser? Who are you calling a loser? I have the crane with the wrecking ball. I have a team of the ugliest, thugliest men and women of Blackbird Hill ready to move into the Pump Street houses and shops. They are Lady Frankenstone's bailiffs and they will take out all the things the Pump Street people own. They will load them onto lorries and vans and take them to Blackbird Hill where there are empty houses waiting for them. Then – before this day is out – the wrecking ball will start its work. So, stick that in your gunpowder barrel and smoke it.'

There was a rumble of diesel engines as five large lorries and vans trundled along the road from Blackbird Hill. The drivers and crews were every bit as horrible as Igon had said. Ugly, warty faces stared through the windscreens; their hairy faces hadn't been shaved for a week. And that was just the women. The men weren't so bad.

Guy Fawkes's Yorkshire smile grew wide as a Yorkshire pudding[33]. 'Aye, lad, line them up. That's perfect.'

'Perfect?' James King the crane driver said. 'Perfect for what?'

'We can take all the lorries and vans out along with the crane.'

Igon shook his head. 'Take them out with what?'

Guy Fawkes pointed to the large glass window of a building facing the Town Hall. Boy stood there and waved. In his hand was a smartphone. 'That lad is at Wildpool swimming pool. He has

---

33 This is quite possible. There are some people who can put a whole Yorkshire pudding into their mouth. They say it tastes batter that way.

a button on his phone. If he presses it, he will set off a small charge that will blow open the valves of the pool. A wall of water a metre high will roll down the street and swamp the engines of all your motors. You won't be able to move for hours.'

The thugly men and women turned and hurried towards their trucks. 'No, no, *no*,' Guy shouted. 'You don't understand. If one person tries to move one vehicle, Boy will set off the charge. Leave them where they are, and they'll be safe. Now just go home.'

The baffled bailiffs trudged back to Blackbird Hill.

'He can't stand there for ever,' James King said.

'He can stay there long enough for the Ladies Who Crunch to come up with a new plan.'

The ladies he spoke of had returned to their seats outside the Top Coffee Café.

'So,' Marjorie Doors said as she picked up her knitting. 'What do we do next, Edna?'

Edna's face was grey as the cobbles in Dank Alley. She whispered, 'I don't know.' She turned watery eyes towards her friends. 'Sorry, Minnie. I've run out of ideas.'

Oh, dear.

I like a nice piece of cod, myself

Lady Frankenstone had not run out of ideas. She had been looking down from her office in Loaf Tower as Boy and the Ladies Who Crunch and Guy Fawkes had foiled her fiendish plot.

As soon as Igon returned to the tower, she began to plot. 'Come into my office, Igon.'

'Your fiendish plot is foiled, Frankenstone. What next?'

'I am full of fiendish plots, little man in black. Frankenstone Castle's Chamber of Monsters will make us millions, Igon. Millions.

People will flock to see our monsters. But we must beat Dr Wiggott. We need to open before he does.'

'He has his infinit-G device and he has *your* infinit-G device. We just have one monster – the man with the bolt through his neck. And even he is a bit too friendly.'

'Then we must turn him evil. I'll give him lessons . . . and we will turn Frankenstone Castle into his lair.' She waved a hand around her office so that Igon could picture the scene. 'Did you see the way the crowds gathered for Guy Fawkes? When they all thought that little girl was going to be blown up?'

'Yes, my lady.'

'Then that's what we'll offer the Wildpool crowds. They will pay to come into Frankenstone Castle.'

'You want our monster to blow up a little girl?'

The lady's red lips turned down in disgust. 'Don't talk as stupid as you look, Igon. My monster must threaten the little girl and every child in Wildpool. Tell them that if we don't stop him, he will bring terror to every person in the town. People love terror more than they love fish and chips.'

'I like a nice piece of cod, myself,' Igon said, and smacked his thin lips. He rolled his eye as if it were a heavenly thought.

'Igon.'

'Yes, my lady?'

'Shut up.'

Igon shut up.

'The monster will be on the loose. One hero will rush forward to rescue the child ... that hero will be you, Igon. But the hero will be dashed aside by the monster's huge and hairy arms.'

'If he's holding the little girl he'll only have one arm free,' Igon said.

'All right, all right.' Lady Frankenstone was breathing loudly as her temper rose. 'You – the hero – will be dashed aside by the monster's huge and hairy *arm*. But the brave villagers will march to the rescue.'

'What villagers?' Igon asked.

'Our friends from Wildpool. The ugliest and thugliest people in Wildpool will lead the visitors who will join the action. The crowds will cheer as they snatch the little girl and save her. Word will get around. People will travel from all over the country to see this show every night... Once we clear a new road through Pump Street.'

'But the boy says he'll release a flood of water as soon as the drivers start to move. How will you stop him?' Igon asked.

'I'm glad you asked me that,' his boss replied. 'I have the answer.'

'I thought you might,' Igon said. 'And I bet you a plate of cod and chips that it's an evil plan.'

'Oh, Igon it is. So wicked I almost shock myself.' And Lady Frankenstone cackled like a witch in a very bad movie[34].

---

34 Except she didn't have a broomstick. Or a black pointy hat. Or a black dress. Or broken teeth. Or a pointy chin. Or a black cat. Or matted grey hair. Or warts on the end of a long, pointed nose. Apart from *those* things she cackled like a witch.

I don't
do nice

'We will wait till that boy has gone to sleep. Then we shall drive up Pump Street and knock it down.'

Igon frowned. 'But ... if Boy is asleep ... then everyone in Pump Street will be asleep.'

'So? So? So what?'

'So, you'll be knocking down cottages with people asleep inside them. You'll kill them all,' Igon moaned. 'Even I am not that wicked. You'll be arrested.'

'Hah,' her ladyship sneered. 'I'll say that I only sent in the wreckers because the mayor gave the orders. It's the mayor who ordered the wreckers to flatten Pump Street to make way for the new road.'

'But you *are* the mayor,' Igon reminded her.

The lady in red looked pained. 'Oh, Igon, Igon, Igon. You need to be eviller if you're going to work for me.'

'I know,' the man sighed. 'I've tried.'

'Then try harder, Igon. Try harder. Think evil and think hard.' She pulled a sheet of paper from her desk drawer. 'Forget the flattening of Pump Street for the moment.' Lady Frankenstone sighed. 'Let's plan the show.'

'I like a nice show,' Igon nodded, eager.

'It won't be a nice show. I, Lady Frankenstone, mayor of Wildpool, don't do nice. It will be a thriller. It will make Dr Wiggott's pathetic history scenes look as dull as dishwater—'

'Ditch-water.'

'What?'

'Ditch-water... Most people say dull as ditch-water, not dishwater.'

She brought her face near to Igon's. 'I do not care what *most* people say, little man. I am *not* most people. I am me. I am the Special One. I am different. So, I will say dishwater if I want... and you will end up *in* ditch-water if you argue with me again.'

Igon sniffed. 'I was only trying to be helpful.'

'Don't[35]. Now, back to my plan... One. We kidnap a little girl.'

'No need to do that,' Igon said. 'That little girl in pink – Araminta – would love to do it.'

Lady Frankenstone nodded. 'Cross off number one, then.' She scribbled through the mark she'd just made on the page.

'Number two...'

'Number one,' Igon said.

'What?'

'You crossed out number one, so your number two becomes your number one.'

'Igon.'

'Yes, my lady?'

'Shut up. Where was I?'

'Planning the thrilling scene of the monster

---

35 This is very good advice. There are some people who think they are *always* right. Not *just* when they are wrong, but *especially* when they are wrong. Don't be helpful to these people. They won't thank you for it.

kidnapping a little girl,' Igon said sulkily. (That's because he was sulking.)

'Then I shall begin,' she promised and began writing furiously.

How could I start a fire when I was thirty leagues away?

Of course, you are wondering how Molly and PC Elloe are getting on in Nero's Rome. Molly was looking on as the great men of Rome prepared to question the emperor about the fire. Constable Elloe was looking for the girl and hoping he'd find her before the rest of Rome did. Tricky.

Molly watched as a general of the Praetorian Guard walked to a platform at the end of the

Senate and blew loudly on a trumpet. Everyone fell silent. The general announced, 'My lords, the Senate has the honour of greeting Nero, Emperor of Rome.'

Everyone turned to look at the platform. Molly couldn't see through the crowds of people. She gave up trying and listened.

Nero spoke in a clear high voice, as sweet and smooth as honey. 'Gentleman. Greetings from your emperor. These are tragic times for our great city. The fire has left so many homeless, some dead, and some with a bit of a nasty cough. Our hearts go out to the families who have lost loved ones.' He gave a little sob as if he really cared for the poor.

There were grumbles rather than pity from the powerful men. 'And who started the fire? That's what we want to know,' someone cried out.

'Aye,' the brave ones nodded. 'Was it you, Nero? That's what they're saying.'

Nero laughed, a treacly chuckle. 'I have heard the foolish stories. They are nonsense.'

Molly heard Master Valerius' voice raised.

'Then, Emperor, is it true you had your servants start the fire for you?'

'I swear by almighty Jupiter that no servant of mine started this dreadful fire.' And *that* was true. It always pays to tell the truth ... unless it is likely to get you into even more trouble.

'You came here a year ago and asked us to knock down many streets to build your new palace,' Valerius went on. Some of the men started to nod and stroke their beards[36].

Nero replied, 'Ah, yes. A golden palace that will be the wonder of the world. It will bring glory to Rome. I know. People think that is why I started the fire.' Nero's voice was rising – a little bit of anger and a lot of panic. 'But I was in my summer house over in Antium when the fire started. Ask my servants. How could I start a fire when I was thirty leagues away?'

By now Nero was practically screaming and some of the lords had started to cheer. Nero jumped up to a higher platform and punched his fist in the air. Molly could see him properly for the first time. 'Go out there and find the *real* fire

---

36 They stroked their beards if they had them. The ones who didn't have beards had to stroke their chins instead. You can try it yourself. It makes you look ever so clever – even if you're not – and even if you don't have a beard.

raisers,' he cried. 'Find the red-haired girl I saw at the—'

Nero stopped and choked as if he'd swallowed his runaway tongue. 'I mean, that my servants reported. A Celt with red pigtails. Find the girl and we can all enjoy seeing her thrown to the gladiators in the arena just like the Christians.'

'Will she get a fair trial?' Valerius asked.

'Hah,' the emperor sneered. 'I'd bet she *is* a Christian. *That* is against the law. She doesn't need a trial.' Nero's mad eyes were wild and wide. 'A nasty nest of traitors from the East. They call themselves Christians. Seek them out. Bring them to me and I shall destroy them. Destroy them all. My lions and bears and boars and bulls are waiting in the arena. My Roman friends, let us watch them bleed and suffer for our sport.'

And the thought of the cruelty turned the Roman lords to cheering. That was the moment when Emperor Nero looked around. He looked at the sea of smiling faces. The crowd parted for a moment. He saw one small face that was pale and shocked. He saw Molly.

Oooops.

Hi-ho, Silver, away!

Nero's face turned to one of cunning. He raised an arm. 'There is a Christian spy here in our Senate. Seize her.' He pointed straight at Molly, standing half-hidden by Lord Valerius.

Molly was used to escaping angry enemies – and none had been angrier or more enemified than Arfur Loaf of Loaf Tower. Before the Roman people could turn she was weaving between the legs of confused senators. The powerful men grabbed hold of Master Valerius who squawked, 'Not me ... I swear ... not me ... spare me, Nero, spare me!'

'Not him,' the Emperor cried. 'Let me, Nero your lord – Nero the Roman god – let me find this spy and capture her. Out of my way!'

Nero jumped off the platform and the crowd parted to let him through.

Molly burst through the crowd into the Forum. Twenty metres away she saw PC Elloe. For once his brain was working fast ... faster than treacle pudding off a greasy spoon. 'Run, Molly, run! There's a horse over there!' he cried and pointed. In the dizzying race she thought the policeman was pointing at Master Valerius's donkey.

Molly was at the top of the steps leading down to the road. 'If I ran any faster I'd be flying,' she panted. She reached the donkey and began to unfasten it from the black horse it was tied to. PC Elloe sprinted across the Forum to reach her. 'I'll never get far on the donkey,' she groaned as she struggled with stiff leather straps.

'So, take Nero's chariot,' PC Elloe urged. Then he blushed. 'I can't believe I am telling a thief to do some thieving,' he sighed.

'The emperor's chariot?' Molly gasped. 'I can't drive.'

'I can only drive with L-plates,' the policeman said. He looked up and saw the crowd moving towards them. Nero pushed his way to the front.

'Give yourself up, Celt girl. You have no chance. Give yourself up quietly and I'll make sure you die quickly.'

Molly muttered, 'He's so kind.'

PC Elloe had climbed aboard the chariot and grabbed the reins. He reached down and pulled Molly up alongside him.

'I've seen them in the Circus Maximus. It looked easy enough[37]. . .' Molly said as she climbed aboard. Nero had reached the top of the steps now. 'Now's the time to try it.'

She took the reins from PC Elloe in one hand and held the whip in the other. The whip cracked, the black stallion reared up, pawed the air, leapt forward and scattered the crowd.

The charioteer was running down the road clutching a sausage.

'Stop that chariot!' he wailed.

'Stop that chariot!' Nero echoed. He stood on the top step with his general alongside him.

---

37 That was true. Except for the ones that crashed, of course. We'd better not remind Molly of those.

'I have a racing chariot parked behind the Senate, Highness,' the general offered.

'Fetch it, General. Then let's catch the villain and make her an example to the whole of Rome. No one nicks Nero's nag and gets away with it.'

The general was a hard and dangerous man. He jogged out of sight and returned a moment later with a racing chariot harnessed to a white horse. Nero climbed up and snatched the reins from the general. 'I can drive, Highness,' the general offered.

But Nero giggled and screamed, 'Hee. I've always wanted to do this. Hi-ho, Silver, away!' He cracked the whip. The stallion stood quietly. 'I said, "Hi-ho, Silver, away!"' The horse remained still.

The general cleared his throat. 'Sorry, Highness. His name's not Silver, Highness.' He whispered the name of the horse in the emperor's ear.

An Elloe's word is his bond

Nero was furious. 'I can't stand here, in front of my Roman people, and shout, "Hi-ho, Fluffy, away!"'

'It's the horse's name. You must call him by his name. The slave will escape, Highness,' the general muttered.

Nero hissed, 'You do it.'

The general shrugged. 'Hi-ho, Fluffy, away!'

The white stallion reared up and set off at such a pace Nero was thrown over the back of the chariot. He clung to the back rail as the chariot hurtled through the ruined streets. The general hauled the emperor back onto the chariot floor clumsily. Nero dusted himself down and set his crown straight.

'I was about to say, "You do it … when I *say* so,"' he raged.

'Sorry, Highness.'

Molly's chariot was out of sight, but the wheels had left a trail in the ashes that the emperor could follow. As Molly and PC Elloe sped along, Molly looked over her shoulder while PC Elloe checked his stolen map[38]. 'Once we get past the Circus Maximus we can take the back streets to where we came in,' the policeman shouted over the noise of the clattering hooves and the rushing air.

'How far, Constable?' Molly panted, and her shoulders ached as she steered the powerful horse clear of the soot-stained rubble by the side of the road.

'Past the Circus Maximus then it's five hundred metres to the Tiber gate.'

The huge arena loomed in front of them. The east wall was ruined but the wind had taken the fire away from the rest of the building and

38 A top tip from Molly there. Don't think and drive.

three sides stood tall as ever. The black horse galloped alongside the crumbling arena wall. Molly looked around the tumbling houses on the other side of the road where blackened people were scrabbling in the smoking ashes to see what was left of their lives. 'Look at Rome. All wicked Nero's work,' she said.

Suddenly PC Elloe cried, 'Look out.'

While Molly had been looking over her shoulder a troop of soldiers had been marching down the street. They blocked the way ahead. The girl turned the horse sharply and the chariot-horse swerved the only way it could . . . through the ruined gates of the Circus Maximus.

The racing track was not damaged, though some rows of seats in the east stand were burned out. 'We're trapped,' Molly groaned, ready to jump down and run.

'No,' PC Elloe said quickly. 'Let's wait in here till the soldiers are gone. . . And Nero has ridden past. We are safe here, Molly Maltby, safe. I said that PC Elloe would keep you safe and an Elloe's word is his bond.'

'What does that mean?' Molly asked as the black horse slowed to a jog around the race-track.

The policeman shrugged. 'I don't know what it means. It was something my dad used to say.'

At that moment, outside the arena, Nero in the racing chariot came across the troop of soldiers and drew to a halt. 'Has a chariot driven by a young slave come this way?' he demanded.

The centurion in charge hadn't seen Molly's sharp turn. 'No, sir. Not that we've seen.'

So maybe PC Elloe was right. Maybe they really *were* safe. But then again...

Yes, I like that.
A race to the death

Nero raised his fists to the skies. 'Ye gods. How could you do this to *me* – a fellow god?' he asked. He turned to the general of the Praetorian Guard and said, 'They must have turned down one of those side streets. We'll never find them.'

'I'll send out searchers, Highness,' the general offered. His face was hard as the chariot wheel, yet his eyes showed something else – disgust for the gold-crowned man who stood beside him.

Nero groaned. 'I would so like to have captured them like a hero. Nero the Hero.'

'Shall we drive back to your palace, Highness?' the hard-faced general asked.

'Yes...' Nero began. Then, 'No. No. Did you know I have ridden in the Circus Maximus many times[39]?'

'Yes, Highness. And won every time.'

'I did indeed. But I always thought they ... they *let* me win, me being emperor and all that ... and me wanting to execute anyone who beat me. I never *enjoyed* winning,' the emperor wailed. He was close to tears.

'I'm sure you won because of your skill, Highness,' the general said carefully.

Nero looked a little brighter. 'You think so? Then let me show you how good I am. Let me take you for a spin around the Circus Maximus.'

'As you wish, Highness,' the general replied with a small bow of the head. He turned the chariot into the arena gateway.

As they drove into the ruined arena Nero's face split into a grin as wide as a Roman sewer ... the ones where they threw the bits of Nero's victims.

39 Did you know, Nero was a winner at the AD 67 Olympics – even though he lost? He rode in the ten-horse chariot race ... and fell off. They gave him the prize because he said, 'I would have won if I hadn't fallen off' and ... because they were so scared of what he'd do to them if they didn't let him win. Top tip: next time you lose a game, try that excuse: 'I would have won if I'd played better. Give me the prize.'

He looked up the skies. This time it was to praise his friends, the gods. 'Oh, the great god Jupiter is smiling on me today. You have delivered me the little spy-girl herself.'

Molly looked like a trapped rat in a cage. Nero's chariot blocked the way out. Even if she jumped down and ran there was no way to the outside and freedom. Nero smiled and turned to the general and said, 'Kill her.'

The general drew his sword and its shadow fell over the face of the girl.

Suddenly PC Elloe spoke up as he stood at Molly's side. 'You'll have to catch us first.'

'What?' Nero asked. 'What did you say?'

'He means we're not going to stand here and let that soldier cut us down,' Molly said.

Nero's face turned bright as his silver crown. 'Ooooh... A race is it? Yes, I like that. A race to the death. Three laps of the track.' His laugh was as cold as the ashes on the track.

No, foolish girl. This is how real racers turn!

'It's our only chance,' PC Elloe said.

Molly nodded and called across to Nero, 'If we win, we go free?'

Nero nodded. 'And if I win I throw you to the lions tomorrow[40].' Nero spoke from the side of his mouth to the general, 'If I lose, kill her anyway. The girl is too dangerous to live.' But Molly's sharp ears heard the chilling words. Nero spoke brightly, 'One rider in each chariot... get down, General.'

The soldier stepped down slowly and led his emperor's chariot to the starting line. PC Elloe

---

40 Better to be thrown to the lions tomorrow than chopped up and thrown in the sewers today, I always say.

did the same for Molly. Nero's chariot stood alongside the girl's. 'General, raise your sword. When you bring down the sword, that is the signal for us to start,' Nero commanded.

Molly's black horse moved up to the sooty starting gates. The general raised his sword. Nero's eyes glinted madly. PC Elloe felt as if he'd been holding his breath for five minutes.

The general lowered his sword. Molly cracked her whip and the black horse leapt forward. Nero cracked his whip over the white horse ... and nothing happened. He roared with anger.

'Ohhhh, ye gods,' he groaned, then shouted, 'Hi-ho, Fluffy, away!'

The white horse jumped forward so rapidly Nero was thrown over the back of the chariot again, and had to cling on to a rail as he'd done before. He spent the first length of the stadium struggling to climb back aboard while Molly surged well ahead. At last Nero was back in the chariot. He sighed with satisfaction. 'Ahhhh.' Then he saw the end wall looming. 'Ahhhh,' became, 'Argggghhhh.'

Nero's white horse swung around the western

turning post and the spinning force threw him over the side. Again he was clinging to the rail as his legs flew outwards. As the horse headed up the back straight for the first time he pulled himself aboard, gathers the reins and was back in control.

Molly looked back over her shoulder and turned at the eastern turning post to complete the first lap. Her black horse was cantering. 'Faster, lad, faster,' Molly urged.

'Faster, Molly, faster,' PC Elloe cried.

Molly rushed past the starting line where the constable stood, and the general turned a score marker calling out. . . 'One lap.'

Nero skidded around the eastern turning post in a cloud of dust, cheering himself wildly. 'Go, Fluffy, go.'

As Molly reached the western turning post for the second time Nero was closer. Molly carefully guided her chariot around.

Nero laughed, 'No, foolish girl. This is how real racers turn. . .'

The emperor threw the chariot into a side-skid and spun around the turn. As they headed east on the back straight for the second time Nero drew level.

'You are dead, slave, dead!' he screamed. And Molly believed him.

Bring in the sweet little child

The windows of Loaf Tower were a grey smoked glass. The skies above Wildpool were a gloomy smoke brown.

Lady Frankenstone put her pen down and looked at the sheet with pride. 'This, Igon, will be the best drama Wildpool has ever seen. Have you found me the girl?'

'Yes, my lady. She is in the next room.'

'Bring in the sweet little child.'

Igon gave a small bow and wondered, 'Why did I do that?'

The girl was in her school uniform of grey but

had pink ribbons in her hair and was wearing pink socks. She was walking up and down the waiting room looking cross. 'I have to be back at school in ten minutes, so make this quick,' she demanded.

Igon held open the door to Lady Frankenstone's office and the girl walked through. The Lady Mayor gave a glittering smile as false as her teeth. 'Good morning, young ... errrrr ... what's your name?'

'Araminta. That's my name and don't forget it.'

'Not a name I'm likely to forget,' the woman replied. 'We are putting on a drama at Frankenstone Castle and we need a girl to play the part of a captured child who tries to make friends with my monster and has to be rescued by the good folk of the town.'

'Good folk? You won't find many of them in Wildpool,' Araminta said, sour as lemons.

'We'll give you an ice cream if you do well,' the mayor promised.

Araminta's pouty mouth fell open. 'What? An ice cream? I am going to be a star and you are offering to pay me in ice cream?'

For the first time in a long time Lady Frankenstone looked unsure of herself. 'What *would* you like, Araminta?'

'How much are you charging for tickets?' the child asked.

'Twenty pounds for adults and ten pounds for children and wrinklies[41].'

'Then I want half,' the little girl said.

'A quarter,' Lady Frankenstone offered.

'A third – and that's my final offer. I am a local hero. Read tomorrow's *Wildpool Gazette*. I am front-page news after I defused that bomb. . .'

'Well, you didn't exactly. . .' Igon began.

'Read the newspaper. That's what the people of Wildpool will believe when they read the paper. They will flock to see me in our monster drama. I will be top of the bill. My name is gold to you and I will make you a fortune. One-third. Full stop. One-third or I walk away from the deal.'

Lady Frankenstone looked faint and clutched at the side of her desk to stop herself falling over.

41 Calling elderly people 'wrinklies' is just a bit offensive. Lady Frankenstone could do it because she was a wrinkly. You can't. Show some respect. Call them codgers or crones, old-timers or old trouts.

'One-third.'

'And I want to see the script and change it if I have to.'

The mayor nodded and passed the sheet of paper across the desk to her.

'Not very neat handwriting,' Araminta said with a sniff. A minute later she said, 'I have one or two changes, but it's quite good.' She stuck out a tiny hand to shake. 'I think we have a deal, Mayor.'

'Oh, good,' Lady Frankenstone said weakly.

Araminta turned to Igon. 'I need time to rewrite the script and rehearse. You can call Wildpool Primary School, tell them you're my father, and say I have Blue Monkey Fever and I'll be off school for a few days.'

Igon said, 'Yes, miss,' and bowed. As he left the office he muttered, 'I'm doing it again. Why am I bowing to a bossy child?'

Good question. No one had the answer.

No one ever sees Dr Wiggott

Across the road from Loaf Tower, in the Top Coffee Café, the Ladies Who Crunch sat in the shadow of the wrecking-ball crane. Boy walked across from the baths to join them.

'Have you taken Guy Fawkes back to Wiggott's Wonderful Waxworld?' Minnie Cooper asked.

'I handed him over to Mr Crudge the caretaker,' Boy nodded.

'You didn't see Dr Wiggott, then?' Marjorie Doors asked.

'No one ever sees Dr Wiggott,' Edna Crudge said quietly.

'He is a dangerous man to have roaming around Wildpool,' Minnie said with a tremble in her voice.

'You think Dr Wiggott is a dangerous man?' Boy asked.

'No-o. Guy Fawkes is a dangerous man,' she said. 'If he'd set that bomb off he'd have caused a lot of damage.'

'He wouldn't,' Edna argued. 'He couldn't. My Billy is working on making new Wiggott's Waxworlds with the infinit-G chip. Models like Guy Fawkes are just gloop with electronic brains powered by a computer. The computer won't let them harm real people.'

'But Guy Fawkes laid a bomb. What if that had gone off?' Marjorie Doors asked.

'The bomb was made of gloop, too,' Edna said. 'If the fuse burned down it would have gone *pop* and we'd have been spattered with a little sticky gloop, that's all[42].'

'Boy here has a bomb in the swimming baths ready to explode and flood the centre of town,' Marjorie argued, her knitting needles flying like an angry war-bird.

---

42 'That's all,' she says? Not everyone can stand being glooped. And the cleaning bill is enormous.

Boy shook his head. 'There's no bomb there.'

'It was a lie?' Minnie asked.

'A bluff. But it worked.' They looked across at the crane and the lorries that were cluttering the road.

'Maybe not for much longer,' Boy said. He took a printed sheet of paper out of his pocket, pushed the coffee cups aside and spread it out. The Ladies Who Crunch leaned forward and read...

**Frankenstone's Monster Live Show
See the famous Araminta kidnapped
Join in the hunt around the grounds of
Frankenstone Castle
Fun and terror for all the family
Wildpool's biggest and bestest attraction ever
(Puts Wiggott's Woeful Waxworld in the shade)
Tonight at 7 p.m.
Adults £20. Children and wrinklies £10.**

'We have to stop it or your Billy will be out of a job,' Minnie said. 'What's our plan, Edna?'

'I told you. I don't have one. Molly Maltby

has the sort of bright young brain we need.' She turned to Boy. 'Did you see Molly when you went to Wiggott's?' she went on.

Boy shook his head. 'It seems she went off into Nero's ancient Rome and was followed by that Constable L.O. Elloe.'

'Ooooh,' Minnie cooed. 'So dangerous there. Nero was batty.'

'No,' Edna said, weary. 'I told you, the new Waxworld figures can't hurt real humans.'

But Minnie frowned. 'Does Molly know that?'

Edna gave a harsh laugh. 'Of course she does.' Her face showed a flicker of doubt. 'She *must* do.' More doubt. 'I'm *sure* she does.'

Minnie shivered. 'I *hope* she does.'

Final lap and the winner is...

Molly was racing for her life. Her black horse was a warhorse, strong and steady. The emperor's white horse was a racing horse, fast and nimble.

'Two laps gone – one to go!' the general shouted as they raced side-by-side.

PC Elloe urged, 'Molly, you have to use the whip.'

She cracked the whip and the horse shot forward so quickly she almost copied Nero's fall over the back of her chariot. By the time she reached the western turning post for the third and final time she was level with the emperor. But the emperor's skid-turn put him ahead again.

On the long back straight Molly caught Nero and they raced neck-and-neck. Nero sneered and steered his chariot sideways so his wheel clashed with Molly's wheel. There was a splintering more painful than a pulled tooth and the girl knew her chariot was damaged.

Nero laughed and threw his chariot into the final eastern turning post. But this time his inside chariot-wheel struck the post. The wheel snapped off the axle. It bounced back down the back straight towards Molly. She ducked and it flew over her head.

Nero's second wheel took the strain and then snapped too so the body of the chariot was dragged for a little, turning to splinters as it slowed to a halt.

Molly guided her damaged chariot around the wreckage of Nero's as the emperor lay groaning and dazed on the sandy track.

The girl's chariot limped over the finish line.

The general shouted, 'Final lap and the winner is ... the emperor.'

PC Elloe gasped, 'The emperor?'

'The spy-girl cheated,' the general went on. 'She barged into the emperor's chariot on the last lap.'

'No. Nero barged into me,' Molly called angrily. 'He lost.'

'The emperor never loses[43].'

The general opened the gate to the outside. The open road to the streets could be seen through it. The general lifted Molly's chariot and pushed the loose wheel back on firmly.

The soldier's face was stone as he said quietly, 'I must help my emperor. He will be very upset if you *escape* while I am helping him.'

Molly grinned at him. 'That would be terrible.'

'Terrible,' the general said. The man turned his back on Molly and strode over to Nero. 'Well done, Highness. You won.'

'I did, didn't I? She cheated, didn't she?'

'She did.'

Nero grasped the front of the general's armour and pulled himself up. 'So, have you executed them?' the dazed emperor asked.

The general crossed his fingers. 'Sadly, I wasn't

---

43 Remember that next time you challenge an emperor to a game of Snakes and Ladders. Emperors are bad losers ... no, *bad* losers

able to. I had to make sure your godly body was safe first, your holiness. As soon as I turned my back the girl and her guard escaped. Now let's get you back to your palace for a long rest.'

But Nero's eyes burned. He gripped the general's breastplate and hissed. 'I need to be at the Colosseum now. My wonderful people will want to see me. So long as that girl is alive, my life is in danger. She knows ... things.'

'Things? What sort of things?'

'Things about me,' Nero said.

'What sort of things about you?'

'Things about me and the Great Fire of Rome that I didn't start.'

The general nodded wisely. 'Oh. *Those* sorts of things.'

You can kill her after I've killed her

P C Elloe guided Molly through the tangle of smoking streets using the map he'd stolen from the blind beggar ... except he wasn't a beggar, he wasn't blind and the constable didn't 'steal' the map.

They came to the place where they'd entered Nero's Rome. Molly couldn't see the railway line, but she knew it was just five paces ahead of her. She took one step. She heard a voice. 'There she is.'

It was Master Valerius. He had with him the driver of the emperor's chariot whose face was purple with anger. 'A runaway slave,' Valerius cried. 'She's mine. The punishment is death.'

'No, no, a chariot thief,' the driver shouted. 'She's mine. The punishment is death.'

Valerius turned to the man furiously. 'I saw her first. You can kill her after I've killed her.' Molly and PC Elloe backed away. Two steps from the safety of Wiggott's Wonderful Waxworld. The driver was too quick. He leapt forward and grabbed Molly's shoulder. As Molly wriggled Valerius took the other shoulder. 'Too late, PC Elloe,' the girl moaned.

Molly struggled and the sudden movement caught her captors by surprise. She pulled them nearer the Waxworld's railway line. 'Just one step from Wiggott's,' the constable urged and tried to pull her to safety.

But suddenly PC Elloe found another pair of hands was dragging him back. 'That's the man who stole my map,' the blind beggar cried. 'And the girl is worth a fortune if I hand her over to Nero.'

It was three against two. The three won ... as they usually do.

Molly and the constable were helpless as flies in a spider's web.

'A fortune?' the driver said.

'Yes,' the beggar explained. 'She's the spy that Nero has been searching for.'

'Good.' The driver nodded. 'I caught her; I get the reward.'

'She's my slave. I own her, so I should get the reward,' Master Valerius said.

For a while they bickered and bartered and at last agreed they would share the reward for Molly equally. Master Valerius said, 'The emperor will be on his way to the Colosseum now. He always goes there at this time of day.'

'Perfect,' the driver said, rubbing his hands together. 'We'll take them to the Colosseum and Nero can reward us in front of all those people.' He took some of the reins from the chariot horse and used them to bind the hands of the prisoners. Their captors marched PC Elloe and Molly ahead of them down the sooty road till the massive arena loomed over them.

'Nice place,' PC Elloe said.

Molly shook her head. 'It's a place where

tens of thousands of animals and humans died horribly and fifty thousand cruel Romans watched for fun.'

The young policeman nodded. 'Not such a nice place then.'

The cleverest girl in Wildpool saw herself dying as a lion's dinner in Rome[44].

---

44 When someone young dies, it's said they 'died before their time'. Molly would die about two thousand years before her time.

Ashamed of yourself, you should be. Ashamed!

Boy entered Dank Alley and the rats squeaked their welcoming squeaks before vanishing down the broken drain covers. He reached the sign that said, *Deliveries – Knock three times*.

He knocked three times and waited. Billy Crudge seemed to take a long time to answer. After several minutes Boy finally heard the door creak open and Billy Crudge gave his usual miserable welcome. 'Oh, it's you.'

'Nice to see you too, Mr Crudge.' The boy-thief sniffed loudly at the musty air. 'It does smell fresh in here today, Mr Crudge. I wonder why that is? I *know*. You must have had a bath – have you?'

Billy Crudge's cheeks showed red patches as his blood boiled. 'If you've come here to insult me you can get out. Go on. Get out now before I take my broom to you,' he said and rattled an old brush that had been leaning against his office wall.

'I'm shaking with fear, Mr Crudge.' Boy stretched out a hand and wiggled it. 'Oo-errrr. See what you've done to me. Made me shake with fear.'

'My wife took you in off the streets of Wildpool. Off the very streets when you ran away from that evil school. And how do you repay her? You come here just to make fun of her husband. Ashamed of yourself, you should be. Ashamed!'

Boy didn't look very ashamed. 'Talking of Mrs Crudge ... who saved me from a life on the streets of Wildpool... She sent me with a message.'

Billy Crudge turned suddenly pale. 'Edna sent you? With a message? What have I done wrong this time?'

Boy smiled. 'Nothing, Mr Crudge. She needs the help of Molly Maltby to stop the Frankenstone Castle show tonight. She just wondered how much longer Molly would be in Dr Wiggott's Roman World?'

The caretaker shrugged. 'Who knows? Time moves at a different speed in the Waxworlds. You can think you've spent a week in there, but you step out and there's just an hour gone in the real world[45].'

'That's the way it worked in the old Waxworld. But it was dangerous. People really disappeared without a trace in there. That's why you had to close down. But these new models – the infinit-G models made of gloop. Are they safer now?'

'Safe as houses ... at least safer than Minnie Cooper's house'll be when the wrecking ball gets started. Come into the workshop and I'll show you.' He led the way to a black door in a black wall – almost invisible if you didn't know it was there. Inside lights hung over a table where the

---

45 No, that is *not* as daft as you think. We have all sat through maths lessons in schools that seemed to last 27.4 hours. The bell rings and you are amazed to find that, in the world outside the classroom, only an hour has gone by. My record was 47.85 hours in a one-hour history lesson.

figure of Guy Fawkes lay, lifeless now. 'I am going to use his gloop to make a new model... I think Dr Wiggott wants a scene with Ghengis Khan raiding a town.'

'So, where is Dr Wiggott?' Boy asked.

Billy looked at him sharply. 'No one gets to see Dr Wiggott.'

'You do.'

'I'm different. Now, I was going to show you the computer. This controls every model in the Waxworlds. They can't harm a human because the computer won't let them.'

'Safe as houses, as you say. Minnie Cooper was worried.'

'Minnie was born worried, went to school with me and Edna and worried her way through school and life.'

'I'll tell Minnie how safe the worlds are. But what can I tell Edna about Molly?'

The old man sighed. 'Let's jump on the train and have a look, shall we?'

'Good idea,' the boy-thief said. They stepped into the little train and rattled off into the Waxworlds. The green light shone on the front of the locomotive to show the way. Small blue bulbs shone overhead like stars.

For now...

Wolves howl in Frankenstone woods

Lady Frankenstone led the way out of Loaf Tower. The guard at the door tried to make himself a centimetre tall in the hope she wouldn't see him. For someone that large it is always hard to shrink to less than five centimetres.

The woman in red stopped so suddenly Igon almost bumped into her back. She looked out onto Wildpool's greasy streets and spoke quietly – she could have been speaking to the nearby crow that was tearing away at an empty chip wrapper. 'I know you are there, Brian Popplecrump. I know what you did. I will deal with you later. You will not enjoy *that*, Guard Popplecrump.'

For a large man his voice was suddenly squeaky. 'No, your ladyship.'

She placed a red-soled shoe on the pavement and strode off as Igon scuttled to keep up with her. She marched past the lorries and the wrecking-ball crane. 'Get those moved up to the castle for tonight's show,' she ordered.

'But the bomb in the swimming baths...'

'There is no bomb in the swimming baths. It was a lie. A bluff. And those Blackbird Hill zombie-brain-lorry-drivers believed it. Get them to move them.'

'Yes, my lady.' Igon made himself busy with his mobile phone as Lady Frankenstone marched on up the hill. The road twisted and narrowed, and buses and cars were tangled in a jam every fifty metres. The lorries and wrecking-ball crane ground past her and made it all worse. 'This will all be sorted when I build my new road,' she told the little man with the black eyepatch.

She stomped down Pump Street like a general marching in triumph through a conquered city.

The nets at the windows were shabby but clean, doorsteps were worn but scrubbed, doors were old but painted with pride[46]. No more than a hundred people lived in Pump Street, but they were the sort of people you would like to have as friends.

Street lights were flickering on; old lampposts that looked like ancient gas-lamps. Lights were going on in some of the rooms now. Shy faces looked out on a mayor in red walking past their homes. And they knew what she was planning.

The woman in red walked with high heels clacking up the hill towards the castle at the top.

Vans were there, and an army of men and women were unloading heavy equipment. Lady Frankenstone stopped at the gateway to the castle and gave a satisfied smile.

'See, Igon, this is the modern way to do things. Lights and projectors can show the castle in flames, if we want, with the helpless little girl looking out of the castle keep's window. Her piteous cries will tear the night air, as lasers

---

46 Obviously, they were painted with *paint* ... and brushes. You couldn't see inside through the nets at the window, but picture the whitewashed walls with framed and embroidered mottoes over the cosy fireplaces saying, 'Home, sweet home.' I must stop there. The very thought of these poor but honest Pump Streeters being wrecking-balled out is bringing tears to my eyes.

light the skies and eagles soar. Wolves howl in Frankenstone woods over there.'

Igon frowned. 'There are no wolves in this country.'

'Shut up, Igon,' Lady Frankenstone sighed.

A world of fantasy where magical things can happen

'I am painting a picture in sound and light, Igon,' Lady Frankenstone said. 'It will be famous across the world. Millions will pay their money to see it.'

'You'll have to share that money with Araminta and me,' Igon reminded her.

The mayor's eyes narrowed. Her voice lowered. 'Once that pink-ribboned brat has done her job she may have an accident ... the Frankenstone monster may just push her off the roof of the keep to be crushed on the courtyard below.'

'That's evil, my lady.'

The woman shrugged. 'It'll teach her not to be so greedy. Don't feel too sorry for her, Igon. It means more money for you and me, once she's gone.'

'And you call Araminta greedy?' Igon asked in wonder.

'I am in business. I am a good woman and a great mayor. Remember that, Igon. I will bring work to the poor people of Wildpool. I will bring a new road, remember.'

'And you will bring fake wolves to the woods of Frankenstone Castle,' he said.

Lady Frankenstone clapped her hands. 'But that's the thing, Igon. We are no longer in this country with its scruffy little Pump Streets and its dull shops. We are in a world of fantasy where magical things can happen.'

He nodded slowly. 'A bit like Wiggott's Wonderful Waxworld, you mean.'

All the men and women stopped working for a moment as Lady Frankenstone screamed long and loud. 'Aaaagggghhhh. No, you mindless man. Not at all like that boring old dump. The Frankenstone Monster Experience will be a hundred times better. Now go to the castle kitchen and fetch me a cup of tea.'

'Your usual iced tea?' he asked.

'No. Make it as hot as possible. I want it to really, *really* hurt when I pour it over your ignorant little head.' She turned to the woman in charge of the new light and sound fittings.

The woman had dark curling hair under a warm hood. She held sheets of plans in her hand. 'I'm your artistic director. Call me Charlie.' She stretched out a hand to shake. Lady Frankenstone ignored it.

The mayor told her, 'Pleased to meet you, Call-me-Charlie. Turn everything on... I want to see the effect.'

'We haven't had a chance to do final checks yet...'

'Never mind that,' the mayor said as she walked over to a black control panel. 'Is this the main switch?' she asked and didn't wait for an answer. She pulled a large, red lever.

A rainbow of light and sound filled the evening air. Wolves howled, owls screeched and music boomed. Smoke machines belched out a grey mist.

Just for a moment. Then there was a loud bang, and everything went silent and dim.

'What happened?' Lady Frankenstone asked.

Call-me-Charlie said, 'I did warn you we haven't had time to do the checks. You've blown the electrics.'

'Then hurry up and fix them!' the mayor snapped.

'We can't.'

'You blew the electrics; you repair them.'

The woman said, 'You overloaded the system. You've blown the electricity for the whole of Wildpool.' She turned around and looked down on the town in the valley below. A half-moon glowed though the murky air but there was no other light to be seen. 'Only Wildpool Electric Company can repair it now.'

'Oh, bums,' Lady Frankenstone screeched[47].

---

47 I don't know about you, but I am quite shocked by such bad language from a lady – even a lady with red soles to her shoes. If it upsets you then I suggest you do *not* read that line where she says, 'Oh, bums.'

So, they're trapped with all those monstrous characters?

B illy Crudge was annoyed. He had orders from Dr Wiggott to build a new Waxworld of Ghengis Khan and the Mongol hordes, sweeping across the dusty plains of Asia. He had a large tank of gloop ready.

It was an exciting sort of job. It would be a spectacle like no other with horses and armoured warriors, a city to be raided and burned, citizens fleeing and hiding their treasures, temples trashed as priests panicked. Waxworld visitors could step into the story and feel the fears, yet be completely safe. Dr Wiggott's computer would make sure no harm came to the humans.

Now he had to stop work to take this Boy to see Nero's Roman World, just because Minnie Cooper worried and bossy Edna ordered it. The Roman World was up and running. It was fine and dandy, hunky-dory, nifty, neat and first-rate. For Billy Crudge, the greatest adventure was always the 'next' one.

Then there was a soft *clunk*. The green light on the front of the locomotive died and the blue electric stars went out. The train rolled to a halt.

'What happened?' Boy asked.

Billy was cross. 'What happened is obvious, Boy. There has been a power failure. A fuse has blown somewhere.'

'So, we have to walk back to your workshop and fix it?' Boy asked.

'Could be tricky. I've left my torch in the office,' Billy groaned.

Boy snorted. 'No one uses torches these days.' He pulled out his mobile phone and turned on the light. 'Let's get this sorted. Mrs Crudge will be wondering what's happened to me.'

They climbed out of the train and began to walk back down the track through the darkness as heavy as a lead curtain. The Waxworld fuse-box was beside the office door. Boy held the torch as Billy Crudge opened it and looked inside. 'Oh, dear,' the old man said. 'Nothing wrong. I wired it up myself a couple of months ago.'

'Of course there's something wrong,' Boy argued. 'There's no electricity.'

Billy grew angrier. 'I mean there's nothing wrong with Wiggott's electrics. The fault's outside, probably at the power station. The whole of Wildpool must be off.'

Boy shone his torch around the office and the light landed on the computer. The lights on its screen were out. Boy's mind raced. 'You said the computer controls the characters in Nero's Roman World? It stops the figures harming the real humans?'

'Yes, it does.'

'But the computer's off. There's *nothing* to

stop the evil characters hurting Molly and PC Elloe now, is there?' He turned to the door. I need to get into Roman World and see if they need help.'

'You can't,' Billy groaned. 'With no power the gateway won't open. No one can get in or out[48].'

'So, they're trapped with all those monstrous characters?' Boy wailed. 'All I can do is get to the power station and see if I can help. Molly and the copper could be in real danger.'

'Calm down,' Billy said ... though he didn't feel calm himself. 'They may be having a really good time, swimming in Roman baths or having a meal of roasted dormice and flamingo brains in Nero's palace. They may not be in any danger at all.'

'May not?'

'*May* not.'

Boy turned and ran out of the Waxworld door into Dank Alley. He puzzled the rats by hissing as he ran, 'Hunky-dory, fine and dandy.'

But you, dear reader, know where we left Molly and PC Elloe. In a place called ...

---

48 No in or out? How would they do the hokey-cokey? They'd never get to shake it all about, would they?

'terrible danger'. So, let's leave Boy to run off to the power station and see how Molly Maltby and PC Elloe are going to be butchered in the Colosseum ... maybe.

I could throw her to bears or lions.

I n Rome the sun beat down on the huge Colosseum and the smell of blood and sweat, animals and leather, grew stronger as Molly and PC Elloe were pushed through a dark, underground passage. Angry animals roared and growled, snapped and howled.

The roars and growls and snaps and howls all said the same thing: 'I want to be out of here and get my revenge on the humans who trapped me and brought me here. I will tear and bite and chew and rip, swallow and wallow in their gore and more. I am not happy. Hear me? *Not* happy.'

Of all the buildings in all the history of all the world, this must have been the cruellest. At last Molly reached the end of the tunnel. A gate of iron bars blocked the path. The murmuring of the crowd grew to a ragged cheer then a roar that out-roared a hundred lions.

'What's happening?' PC Elloe asked.

Molly looked through the bars. Across the sandy arena there were rows of seats. In the centre there was a grand seat of gold with purple cushions. A cloth canopy shaded it from the glare of the midday sun. A man stood in front of it in a white toga with purple edging. He waved to the crowds and they cheered back. He turned to face the barred gate where Molly stood, and she saw his face. 'Emperor Nero,' she shouted over the screams of the crowd outside and the roars on the animals in cages underground.

Master Valerius poked her in the back. 'Time to face your doom, slave-girl,' he said.

'Time for us to get rich,' the chariot driver cried.

'Time for me to get revenge for that map-thief,' the blind beggar gloated, and he reached past PC Elloe to unlatch the iron barred gate.

The sunlight after the dark made Molly blink. The air smelled fresher than underground, but it was hot as a forest fire. They stepped out onto the sand of the arena and the noise of the crowd fell to a quiet murmur. 'Who are this strange pair? What will Nero do to them? Will we enjoy it?'

Molly stood tall and faced her enemy. Nero's eyes glinted with joy. 'The Celt spy,' he told the spectators.

They jeered and booed as Molly stared back at him. PC Elloe looked around the arena. There were high wooden walls between them and the crowd. There was no escape.

Molly raised a hand as if she were an empress and the baffled crowd went quiet. 'I am not a spy. Nero only wants me dead because—'

'Don't listen to her!' the emperor screamed. 'She has been found guilty of being an enemy of Rome ... and you, my people, *are* Rome. She is *your* enemy.'

Molly tried to make her voice heard but the Romans were baying like hounds about to tear a fox apart. Nero shouted, 'I could throw her to bears or lions.'

'Yes-s-s-s.'

'Or, I can flood the Colosseum and send her to swim with crocodiles.'

'Oh, yes-s-s-s.'

'Or I could let a gladiator in with a sword to cut her down.'

'Yes-s-s-s.'

'I am not going to do any of those things.'

The crowd gasped. Some said, 'Ohhhh.' Disappointed. And some said, 'Ohhhh?'

'No,' Nero shouted. 'Your bold emperor – and god – is going to enter the arena and kill her himself. Pass me a sword, General.'

Some said, 'Ooooh.' And some said, 'I say, you chaps, I wasn't expecting that[49].'

---

49 Sounds like someone from a very posh school, if you ask me. What? You *weren't* asking me? Sor-ree.

You want money?
Then beg for it!

Nero took the short, sharp sword from his general and marched down the steps from the royal throne to the wooden safety-wall. Two guards threw open the doors and Nero stepped into the heat of the arena.

At first, he ignored the captives and the three who had captured them. He strutted like an ostrich around the outside of the arena, waving his sword at the crowd and stirring them into cheering. At last he arrived back at the gate to the throne. He threw off his white toga and handed it to a guard. Underneath, he was wearing the tunic he had worn as a chariot racer.

When the chariot crashed it had left his tunic stained and torn. Nero liked that. He felt it made him look like a man of the people. 'I am the people's emperor,' he roared and beat his chest with the flat of the sword. *Thump-thump-thump.* The screeches of the crowd drowned out the little words, 'Ouch. I hurt myself.'

Now he turned his pale and wild gaze on the people in front of him. He pointed at the old man. 'Aren't you Lord Valerius from the Senate?'

'Yes, Highness,' Valerius said.

'Why have you been sent here to be executed?'

'I haven't, Emperor, no!' the man wailed.

Nero called to the guards at the iron-barred gateway to the animal pens. 'Take him away… I'll have him thrown to wild bulls later.'

The emperor moved on. 'Aren't you my chariot driver?'

'I am, my lord.'

'Why have you been sent here? Speeding? Dangerous driving? Drunk in charge of a horse?'

'No, my lord, I am the person who—'

'Never mind,' Nero said. When the guards returned from throwing Valerius into a filthy pen, Nero told them, 'Take this man away. He can fight in a gladiator battle later. Make sure he is armed with a stick of celery and a glass shield.'

The chariot driver was too shocked to protest as he was dragged away to join Valerius. At last Nero stood before the beggar. 'Greetings, oh wonderful Emperor and God of all Rome and her Empire,' the man cried.

'Don't I know you?'

The beggar sighed. 'I was the cook who poisoned the meal that killed your Uncle Claudius, which let you take the imperial throne, Highness. You sacked me.'

Nero smiled. 'Good man. Why are you here?'

'I captured the Celt spy and her guard here,' he said pointing at Molly and PC Elloe. 'People did say there was a reward.'

'There is a reward,' Nero cried happily. Then his face turned sharp and evil. 'The reward is: I will let you live.'

'No money?'

'Guards, throw this cook onto the streets.'

Nero turned to the man. 'You want money? Then beg for it!'

The beggar smiled. 'Begging beats being bait for bears ... like you're going to be,' he said to PC Elloe, then walked away whistling.

The emperor turned to the constable. 'I have no argument with the spy-girl's bodyguard. You can go too.'

PC L.O. Elloe threw out his chest and said, 'I will never desert a citizen of Wildpool in her hour of need. If you wish to kill Miss Maltby, you will have to kill me first[50].'

Nero shrugged. 'Fair enough,' he said, and raised his sword for the first blow.

---

50 How brave is that? Very brave. Extremely brave. Massively brave. And hugely stupid, if you think about it.

A sensible decision, sir

Boy raced through the dark streets of Wildpool. Rats scurried out of his way, as their eyes glowed red in the light of his phone. People came to their doors to see if the whole town had turned dark. It had. Candles glowed warm in Wildpool windows as he raced along the towpath by the river.

Boy was panting when he reached the power station and saw a man with a lantern entering the main gates.

'Get the lights back on!' Boy cried. 'It's a matter of life and death.'

The man was old, and his face was wrinkled like a cabbage ... except he had a straggly white beard not at all like a cabbage. 'I will do it as soon as you stop chattering and let me get on.'

Boy followed the gnome with the face of a (hairy) cabbage into a control room. It smelled of electricity and burning. 'Master switch has tripped,' the old man said. 'Must have been a massive power surge for some reason. I bet it's that show they're putting on at Frankenstone Castle ... used to call it Greystone Castle when I was a lad.'

'So, push the switch back up.'

'Can't do that, can't do that. It will only work if everything at Frankenstone Castle has been switched off. Otherwise it'll just blow my master switch again.'

'We haven't time to go to Frankenstone Castle and find out,' Boy argued. 'Someone could die in the time it takes to run up there.'

'Don't be silly, sonny,' the little man said. 'I have to do things properly. It's more than my job's worth to touch that switch till I've done checks.'

'How long will they take?'

'Half an hour ... an hour, maybe.'

'It's not worth more than *my* job,' Boy said.

'You haven't got a job here.'

'Exactly,' the young thief said. He reached past the hairy cabbage and threw the switch up...

In Wiggott's Wonderful Waxworld the lights came on and the computer came to life. With a few clicks it was back in control of Nero's Roman World. Billy Crudge moved the mouse and pressed a button. The scene in the Colosseum appeared.

Nero stood with a sword over PC Elloe's head...

In Nero's world, Nero frowned. 'How strange,' he said as the sword wobbled and wavered. 'Do you know, I don't think I can quite bring myself to kill you after all.'

PC Elloe nodded. 'A sensible decision, sir. An unlawful killing, under the Queen's Peace, is against the law.'

'It's not against *my* laws,' Nero said gently. 'And if it was, I would change the law.'

'I see your point, sir.'

*

At Frankenstone Castle, the power returned.

A rainbow of light and sound filled the evening air. Wolves howled, owls screeched and music boomed. Smoke machines belched out a grey mist.

Just for a moment. Then there was a loud bang, and everything went silent and dim.

'What happened?' Lady Frankenstone asked[51].

The woman in charge, Call-me-Charlie, spoke in the darkness, 'We blew the electrics for the whole of Wildpool ... again. I think we need to start switching things off before they try to put the power back on.'

In Wiggott's Wonderful office the computers went dead, and the lights went out. Again.

---

51 Oh, come on, Lady Frankenstone, work it out! Is your brain made of gloop?

It stops my trousers
from falling down

In Nero's Roman Waxworld, Nero shivered. 'Ah, I feel better. I don't know what came over me. I find I *can* kill you after all.'

'Oh, good,' PC Elloe said[52].

In Wildpool Power Station, the hairy cabbage-faced little engineer raged, 'I *told* you to leave this to me.'

But Boy wasn't listening. Boy wasn't even

---

52 'No, no, no,' I hear you cry. You can see PC Elloe's problem. He is just too *polite*.

there. He had run back to the Top Coffee Café. At his side a bunch of keys jangled. They were the keys to Wildpool Power Station. (You have to remember he *is* a thief. A thief with a plan to wreck the Frankenstone attraction and save Wiggott's...)

The crowd in the Colosseum went quiet. They were saving their voices for a great cheer when Nero struck.

Molly stayed calm. She looked at the Policeman. 'L.O. Elloe?'

'Hello?'

'Defend us. I don't have a weapon.'

'Neither do I,' the policeman said.

'I thought I read in the *Wildpool Gazette* that you have a black belt.'

He nodded. 'Yes, it stops my trousers from falling down.'

'I mean a black belt in karate,' she said with a sigh.

The policeman gave a giggle. 'No. The reporter got it wrong. I have a black belt in cookery – one chop and you're dead.'

'You have a truncheon,' she said. 'Hit him over the head.'

Nero looked on angrily. 'You keep out of this, Celt spy.'

'You don't scare me,' Molly laughed.

'Yes, I do,' Nero raged. 'I can kill you painlessly ... or I can kill you in my own time.'

'Hmmm. About eighty years should do,' she answered.

By this time PC Elloe had pulled the truncheon from his belt. He held it in front of him. Nero gave a scream and brought the sword down. The sharp blade dug deep into the truncheon. But it was made of very hard wood and the blade didn't cut through. It just stuck there.

Nero tugged, and Nero pulled, but he couldn't get the blade of his sword free. The emperor raged and kicked out. PC Elloe let go of the truncheon, but Nero couldn't get the blade out of the wood. The sword was useless. He threw it into the sand of the arena.

'Who will rid me of this turnip-headed guard?' he said with a sob in his voice.

A soldier stepped forward and handed the

emperor a spear with a shining and wickedly sharp point.

Nero's face cleared, and a strange grin spread over his face. He raised the spear to his shoulder and took aim.

Molly laughed. 'Nero the Zero,' she said.

'No, I'm Nero the Hero.'

'Nero the Zero Hero,' she said.

'Prepare to die,' the mad emperor hissed.

'Yes-s-s-s,' the crowd cried.

'Prepare to be shocked,' Molly said. She reached across to PC Elloe's belt and pulled out the Taser. She took aim and pulled the trigger.

Two darts shot out with wires on the end and stuck into the front of the emperor's grubby tunic. He certainly looked shocked. He dropped the spear. His eyes stared up to the blue skies. Slowly he fell backwards and raised a cloud of dust.

Molly walked up the quivering Roman god and pulled the darts out, then calmly wound up the wires. The silent crowd was as stunned as their emperor. 'I told you to prepare to be shocked,' she said. She led PC Elloe back to the tunnel that led to the outside. The guards had seen what her Taser could do and they jumped out of her way and let them pass.

Someone in the crowd shouted, 'Wow! Where can I get one of those?'

There's nothing Dr Wiggott can do to stop me

The engineer with the face of a hairy cabbage checked some dials under the light of his torch. 'Demand down,' he muttered. He blew on his wrinkled fingers as though that would bring them luck. He pushed up the main control switch.

Lights went on in Wildpool Power Station. Lights went on in the homes of Wildpool. Power returned to Frankenstone Castle. Call-me-Charlie was careful to switch just a few things on at a time as Lady Frankenstone looked on.

She stood on the castle walls and looked across at the wrecking-ball crane.

'Shall I start knocking down Pump Street now?' James King asked from the cab of the crane.

'No, Mr King. There will be time enough for that later. We have a show to do this evening and you have a part in it. We need Pump Street clear so the people of Wildpool can walk up to see our monster show.'

'And then do I get to flatten the old dump?'

'You do.'

'I can't wait.'

Lady Frankenstone turned to Igon. 'Go back to Loaf Tower and power up the Frankenstone monster. Collect that dreadful little girl on the way back. But hurry. We have an hour before the crowds arrive and we need to practise the action.'

Igon nodded and jogged down the stone steps in the castle keep to the courtyard. He had to dodge the sound and light operators who were laying cables and carrying speakers and projectors. They were covering them with grey cloths, so they looked like the castle stones. The sounds and lights would seem to appear by magic, not by machine.

It really could be the greatest show Wildpool had ever seen. It really could force Wiggott's Wonderful Waxworld out of business.

The mayor looked across the park outside the keep. 'And that dreadful Minnie Cooper will have her pathetic little house crushed to dust. Ooooh, I'm looking forward to that. And there's nothing Dr Wiggott can do to stop me,' she chuckled[53].

Igon went to the door of Loaf Tower. Brian the Guard was waiting.

'Brian,' Igon said. 'Get up to Frankenstone Castle. Lady Frankenstone wants you to collect money at the front gate.'

Brian replied, 'Halt, who goes there?' and blocked the door with his bulky body.

'Don't be stupid, Brian. You know me. You've seen me every day for the past year.'

'So, what's the password?' Brian asked.

'There's no password. We don't use passwords,' Igon said with a sigh. 'We use electronic passes,' he said and waved a piece of plastic in front of the guard's nose.

---

53 There is an old proverb about being too sure of yourself. I think it is, 'Don't count your chickens before they hatch' ... or it could be, 'Don't hatchet your counts before they chicken.'

'I just invented one,' Brian said proudly. 'That sneaky boy-thief got in, and Lady Frankenstone said we need better security. So I invented a password.'

'What is it?' Igon asked.

'Buttercup,' Brian said. 'It's a good one, isn't it? No one would ever guess it.'

'Well done, Brian. Now, let me in.'

'What's the password?'

'Erm, let me see… Is it… Dandelion? No, no, no, don't tell me… It's … buttercup?'

Brian's chubby face broke into a smile. 'Correct. Enter, friend. That password idea's brilliant, isn't it?'

'Totally brilliant, Brian.'

'They call me Brian Brainbox up at the castle.'

'Do they? What makes you think that?'

'The boy-thief told me.'

Igon groaned. 'Boy is a liar and he doesn't work at the castle. You know that. He lied his way into Loaf Tower to steal things. He wouldn't know what we call you up at the castle.'

'So, it's not Brian Brainbox?'

'No. It's Brian the Bungling Buffoon. Now let me past.'

Brian looked sulky. 'Password?'

'Buttercup.'

'No. I just changed the password to treacle pudding.'

There are other secrets that only Billy Crudge knows

Boy arrived at the Top Coffee Café where the Ladies Who Crunch had been sitting quietly in the evening dark till the lights – and the coffee machines – came back on.

He showed them the keys to the power station. Edna smiled. 'I taught you well, Boy.'

Marjorie Doors huffed. 'I don't see what use the keys to Wildpool Power Station will be.'

'Oh, but I do,' Minnie said with a shy smile and a glance at Edna, who was nodding.

Boy explained the effect the power cut had on Molly's Roman Waxworld adventure. 'She could be in real danger if the power goes down when she's in there.'

'I should have thought of that,' Edna said, and her face was serious as a squirrel's teeth[54]. She rose to her feet. 'Minnie, I am leaving you in charge.'

'Thank you, Edna,' she said, and her small mouth was firm.

'Where are you off to?' Marjorie Doors asked.

'I'd better get to Wiggott's to see if Billy wants any help to get PC Elloe and Molly out of Nero's Rome.'

'What help could you be?' Marjorie asked.

Edna planted her hands on the coffee table and leaned forward till her nose was centimetres from her friend's. 'Marjorie Doors, there are things you don't know about me.'

Marjorie narrowed her eyes. 'I know you teach runaway children like Boy here to rob the rich, to right wrongs and do good in secret ... a bit like Robin Hood and Batman.'

'Yes, yes, yes,' Edna said quietly. 'The only people in Wildpool that *don't* know that are the police. But there are other secrets that only Billy Crudge knows, and it will stay that way.'

---

54 And you don't get much more serious than that. No teeth, no squirrel.

She leaned back, gathered her shopping bags, and set off for Dank Alley and Wiggott's Wonderful Waxworld.

Marjorie Doors looked at Minnie Cooper. 'So, you're in charge, Minnie, are you?'

'I am.'

'Why you and not me?'

'Because it's my house in Pump Street that's going to be knocked down, so Edna knows I will fight to the end to save it.'

Marjorie shrugged. 'I suppose so. And Edna's off to save Wiggott's because Caretaker Billy will lose his job if it closes?'

'Exactly.'

'What do we do first, Captain Cooper?' Boy asked.

Minnie looked across the small market square outside the café. Families were holding the adverts about the Frankenstone's Monster Live Show. Parents were wrapping children against the damp night air now that the sun had set. Chattering children were scared and excited and hopping from foot to foot.

The crowd swirled around then began to head

towards Pump Street and Frankenstone Castle. 'We are going to see this Frankenstone monster show,' Minnie said. 'Let's see what they're up to. Then we can work out the best way to stop them.'

Minnie, Marjorie and Boy set off to join the flow of excited people heading up the hill.

You are Elloe the Fantastic Fellow

Molly and PC Elloe walked through the tunnels beneath the Colosseum and through the sickening animal smells.

Then the policeman stopped. 'These animals are shut up here till Nero orders them to kill people . . . or till he orders gladiators to kill them.' L.O. Elloe felt sick at the thought.

'No, Constable,' Molly said. 'These are just moving models made of gloop. Back in the real Nero's Rome they would have suffered, but not here.'

The policeman nodded. 'Still. . . I'd feel better if we set them free.'

Molly grinned. 'Me too.' As they walked down the rows of cages they pulled back the bolts and let panthers and tigers, lions and bears out of their cages. The animals ignored them. So long as there was power to Wiggott's computers, they couldn't hurt a human.

When they burst out into the streets of Rome there was panic. The people who loved seeing the beasts hunted were being hunted by the beasts. 'Serves them right,' Molly muttered.

As the animals disappeared into the ash-covered streets and through doors into houses, a few Romans grew braver and started to follow Molly and the policeman from the arena. She heard the words, 'Celt' and 'spy' and 'reward' and heard the greed in their voices.

As a gang of ragged men and women began to circle her, Molly stopped. She turned so they could all hear her. 'You are gloop.'

'No, I'm not!' an old toothless woman screeched.

Molly ignored her. 'I am Molly the Magnificent. I defeated the god that calls himself Nero. So, you see, I am greater than a god. And this is my guard, Elloe the Fantastic Fellow. His power pistol brought Nero to his knees.'

'It did, didn't it?' the policeman said, proud of himself.

'Last Tuesday we fought Hercules the demigod and we *beat* him,' Molly boasted.

The crowd shrank back.

'Did we?' PC Elloe asked. 'Are you telling fibs? My mum told me never to tell fibs.'

Molly rolled her eyes[55]. 'Even your mum told lies.'

PC Elloe turned pink. 'No, she didn't.'

'Did she tell you the tooth fairy would bring you money when a tooth fell out?'

'Yes.'

'It's a lie.'

For a moment she thought PC Elloe was going to burst into tears. 'I always found money under my pillow next morning,' he said.

Molly said, 'I am Molly the Magnificent and you are Elloe the Fantastic Fellow until we get out of this place. Back in the real world we can believe in the tooth fairy. Not here.'

The policeman agreed unhappily. They

---

55 I don't mean she rolled them along the ground like marbles. Stop being silly.

walked on. If any of the menacing Romans got too near Molly raised the Taser and they jumped back.

At last they reached the invisible doorway back to Wiggott's Waxworld and stepped through onto the little railway track. Blue stars in the sky lit their way until they reached the train standing on the track where Boy and Billy Crudge had left it after the power cut.

They climbed in and set off. But...

Just at that moment Edna Crudge walked through the back door from Dank Alley into the office of her husband. He was watching a television screen that showed the Roman Waxworld. 'I'm worried about that Molly and the policeman,' Edna said.

Billy turned away from the screen. He shouldn't have done that. It was only for twenty seconds while he spoke to his wife. But twenty seconds was all it took.

'Molly and the policeman are fine. It was a bit scary when she was in the Colosseum and the power failed. The Romans could have really hurt them for twenty minutes.'

'A lesson there, Billy. We need our own power as a back-up.'

'We do.' He turned back to the screen. 'What was I doing when you came in?'

'Shutting the Roman world. We don't want any of those nasties escaping.'

'That would never do, that,' Billy laughed.

The train rattled around the track, carrying Molly and PC Elloe to the back door. If they had really listened, they could have heard another set of wheels behind them.

Following.

Oo-errrr.

If you see him, have him arrested. Understand? Arrested!

Minnie, Marjorie and Boy walked down the High Street then along Pump Street, up the hill and to the gates of the castle wall.

The high stone wall surrounded a large estate of grassland and forests with a river that ran down to Wildpool town below. On a small hill stood the castle itself. Floodlights bathed the walls in Frankenstone red.

Excited crowds queued at the gate where Brian the security guard was taking payments.

Some people tapped their bank cards and walked straight through. The awkward ones paid by cash.

Boy took the smartphones of Minnie and Marjorie and downloaded a special programme onto them. 'Just tap and pay,' he said.

'I don't have much money in the bank,' Minnie quavered.

'The money won't come out of your bank account. It comes out of Lady Frankenstone's,' Boy explained.

'Oh, no,' Marjorie objected. 'That's stealing. You may be a thief, Boy, but me and Minnie aren't.'

Boy laughed. 'It's not stealing. The ten pounds comes from her ladyship's account. Who gets the ten pounds?'

'Her ladyship,' Marjorie said, uncertain.

'Exactly,' Boy said. 'Billy Crudge gave me the app. He says the clever Dr Wiggott built it.'

'So,' Minnie said slowly, 'we aren't exactly stealing Lady Frankenstone's cash ... but she is letting us in for free?'

'She is,' Boy agreed.

'Oh, come on, Marjorie. We can pay her back when we get our pensions next Friday.'

So, the two Ladies Who Crunch marched up to the gate, bolder than brass[56], and tapped their phones to the terminal.

'Accepted,' Brian the guard said. Boy stepped up. 'Here, aren't you the lad who tricked his way into Loaf Tower and lifted Lady Frankenstone's stuff?'

'That was my twin brother,' Boy said. 'He's a problem. He does dreadful things and the family are so ashamed of him. Next time he tries to steal from Lady Frankenstone just call the police.'

'I will, I will.'

Boy raised his voice against the babble of the crowd. 'Ashamed, I say. So ashamed. If you see him, have him arrested. Understand? Arrested. Locked away.'

Brian nodded till his whole body jiggled. 'I will, young sir, I will.'

Boy slapped him on the shoulder. 'Good man. Now give me my change.'

'Change?'

---

56 No, sorry, I don't know why people say, 'Bold as brass.' What is so bold about brass? If you're talking about being showy, flashy, gaudy and garish, then why not gold? 'Bold as gold' sounds good.

'Yes, I gave you a twenty-pound note so I want ten pounds in change,' Boy said. The thief reached into the cash box. 'Don't worry, I've got it,' he said. And he walked through the gateway to join his friends with a pocket stuffed with cash. Edna Crudge would give it to the poor tomorrow. She'd be pleased.

Lasers criss-crossed the sky in a rainbow of colours – red, yellow, blue and violet crissed while orange, green and indigo crossed. Eerie music filled the air mixed with odd cries – human and inhuman.

Scared kids clung to mothers' legs and fathers' arms. Trembling parents hissed, 'It's only sounds and lights. Now get your grubby hands off me . . . you've just been eating ice cream!'

The show was ready to begin. . .

Ooooh, it's the famous Araminta

I n Wiggott's Wonderful Waxworld the little train pulled up and PC Elloe and Molly Maltby stepped out. They were a little weary and were looking forward to a rest. They were not going to get one.

Edna Crudge stepped out of the office and said, 'Minnie needs your help if you're going to save her cottage in Pump Street.'

Molly took a deep breath and said, 'The Ladies Who Crunch have come up with a plan?'

'We have. But it doesn't start till after the great Frankenstone monster show finishes and everyone has gone home. You have time to have a rest and a cup of tea in Billy's office,' Edna said.

'I'm off duty,' PC Elloe said. 'I'd love a cup of tea.'

Edna smiled. 'And Marjorie baked some nice scones. Come in and tell me what happened in Nero's Rome.'

'We could go and see Dr Wiggott,' Molly suggested. 'Tell him to his face.'

The smile slid off Edna's face. 'No one gets to see Dr Wiggott.'

Molly shrugged and followed the others into the office. The Waxworld ride was in darkness apart from the dim lights of the blue stars. The girl froze. She was sure she heard the soft snicker of a horse in the shadows. Then someone shushed it. A hoof tapped at one of the rails and a wheel creaked.

Molly stared hard into the dark tunnel, as if staring would make the sounds clearer[57]. Silence fell ... maybe somebody tripped it up. Molly turned and went into the office. She was asleep before Billy could make her tea.

*

---

57 It doesn't. If it did you could wear glasses to make your hearing better. Use a telescope and you'd hear the Man in the Moon chatting to the Woman in Mars.

At Frankenstone Castle the bright laser lights faded and only the dim red floodlights lit the walls of the keep. From the woods came the sound of a wolf. There was a flash of fake lightning then the crash of thunder. The crowd fell silent.

Suddenly a spotlight the colour of moonlight struck the top of the castle keep. Into the spotlight stepped Araminta in her pink dress and pink ribbons. 'Ooooh, it's the famous Araminta that saved Wildpool from the bomb,' a woman whispered to her daughter.

Marjorie Doors heard that and snapped, 'In fact, it was my friend Minnie Cooper who saved the town.'

The woman glared at her. 'My little girl thinks it was Araminta because that's what she read in the paper and she saw her on the television news before we left the house. If it's in the paper and on the television, it must be true.' (This is not true, but you knew that.)

Marjorie was about to argue but the people around her said, 'Shush,' because Araminta was about to speak.

'Daddy has left me here to play in the old

castle because he's gone to visit Granny. "Be a good girl, Araminta," he said. "I won't be long." I've been picking flowers.'

'Awwww,' the crowd sighed.

'Then Daddy kissed me goodbye ... and that was not very pleasant because his aftershave stinks like cat's wee,' she went on.

From the courtyard inside the keep the mayor's voice hissed, 'That's not in the script, Araminta. Get on with it.'

'Pah,' the girl huffed. A second spotlight switched on, lightning flashed and lit the shambling figure of the monster, lumbering along the top of the keep towards her. Everyone gasped.

Araminta noticed him and smiled. 'Hello, I'm Araminta. Will you play with me?'

The monster didn't say anything, but the girl offered him a plastic pansy. She threw a flower over the wall and watched it drift down. 'See? I can make a parachute. Want to try?'

The monster took a flower and threw it after Araminta's. His eyes glowed with happiness. Araminta threw another. The monster chuckled and threw another. It was a wonderful game. He had never been so happy ... in fact, he had never been happy *at all* since Lady Frankenstone had created him.

Araminta threw another flower. The monster had no flowers left to throw. He picked up Araminta and threw her off the castle walls instead.

The monster was ever so upset

Araminta screamed. She was wearing a microphone and the sound hurt the ears of the audience. 'He wasn't supposed to do that,' Lady Frankenstone, inside the castle, groaned.

'In the movie, the monster threw the little girl into the lake,' Igon said. 'She drowned. The monster was ever so upset.'

'Not as upset as Araminta will be.'

'Will she be hurt?'

'Not at all, you silly, one-eyed man. It won't hurt at all. Well...' she said after a moment's thought. 'Not until she hits the ground.'

But Araminta didn't hit the ground. As she floated down like a pink flower, the wrecking ball on the end of the crane swung into the light. Araminta grabbed the chain that held it and wrapped her legs around it. She ended sitting safely on the huge iron ball. James King the driver lowered her safely to the ground.

The crowd roared. James King stepped out of the crane cab and took a bow. Araminta stomped off. 'And *that* wasn't in the script either. Just wait till I see Lady Frankenstone! I want double-pay for taking risks like that.'

'I saved you, little girl,' James King shouted from the cab of his crane.

'And I saved you when Guy Fawkes planted a bomb under you. We're quits. Now show me the way to the castle door so I can deal with the woman in red.' She stomped off.

'That was amazing!' a child cried. 'Better than anything I've ever seen on television.'

'It was,' his mother agreed. 'That was worth the money.'

'What happens next?'

'Wait and see ... and let go of my leg

234

with your grubby hands. You've been eating chocolate.'

Everyone in the crowd waited to see what would happen next. 'What happens next?' Marjorie Doors asked.

'In the movie, the mayor of the town stands on a platform and orders the villagers to take flaming torches and go out to hunt down the monster,' Minnie explained.

'But the monster's on the castle walls.'

'Oh no he's not,' Boy said quietly. They looked up. The monstrous creature of gloop had disappeared. 'He's on the run[58].'

Lightning flashed and Lady Frankenstone was seen on the top of the castle wall. The crowd gasped. 'It's the mayor. The monster will get her,' they roared.

'Quiet!' the woman shouted. 'The monster has escaped.' Uproar. 'We must find it before it attacks any more children.'

More roars. Then Lady Frankenstone pointed to the castle walls where the ancient black-and-white movie flickered into life. Igon ran around

---

58 Monsters don't run. They lumber, shamble, hobble, plod, clump, trudge and stagger. Sorry, Boy, if you'd spent more time in school you'd be better at using English. Like what I is.

the crowd dividing them into groups as Brian handed out electric torches that looked like the flaming torches in the movie.

The mayor in the film cried, 'Ludwig, you will search the woods!'

Igon shouted to the tall schoolteacher, 'You are Ludwig, and this is your group.' A group of families gathered around him.

'Lady Frankenstone, you will take to the mountains.' Lady Frankenstone was lowered to the ground on the wrecking ball and gathered a group around her.

'I will lead the third group by the lake,' Igon cried, and took the excited families who were left towards the river that ran through the castle grounds.

'Remember, get him alive if you can, but *get* him,' the mayor in the movie shouted. 'The fiend must be found.' And the cheering hordes that remained followed Igon, carrying their torches into the night.

Soon only three people remained. Marjorie Doors, Minnie Cooper and Boy.

'That was amazing,' Minnie said. 'It'll be a huge success.'

Marjorie glared at her. 'Don't let Edna Crudge hear you say that. She wants Wiggott's to be the big attraction in the town.'

Minnie put her hat straight. It had been knocked to one side by the visitors in their excitement.

'But *why* is Edna so keen to see Wiggott's succeed?'

Boy said, 'It's Billy's job.'

'No,' Minnie said wisely. 'Mark my words, it's more than that.'

'What is it?' Boy asked.

'I don't know,' the elderly lady said.

You have faced the most brutal monster the world has ever seen

It took over an hour of hunting the castle's forests and fields, lakes and barns, hills and dales. At last the group led by the teacher discovered the monster in a mountain crevice. They came up with a plan to lure him out then drop a net over him. He was led back to the castle in chains. He stood beneath the main tower.

The other groups were called back to witness the trial – and destruction – of the monster.

The schoolteacher was a hero – even though he had a bad haircut – and Lady Frankenstone took her place on the castle walls to act as the judge.

In Wiggott's Wonderful Waxworld Edna woke Molly and said, 'We are off to see the end of the Frankenstone monster show, then save Minnie's cottage. You can stay here and rest if you like.'

Molly yawned and stretched then said, 'You're not doing this without me.' She rose to her feet and walked to the office door. 'Wiggott's Wonderful Waxworld was still and quiet. There was a faint smell of horse in the air, but no one took much notice[59].

She led the way into Dank Alley, followed by Edna Crudge and her husband Billy. PC L.O. Elloe followed behind. Billy slammed the door and the latch clicked. No one could get in without the key (which was safely in his pocket).

But someone as clever as you will know what

---

59 This could be a big mistake. If you go to your local wax museum, expect to smell candles. If you smell horses, then it's just plain *wrong*. You could check it out. But if it happened to me I would start running and not stop till I was safely tucked up in the top of a tall tree. Not many people know this, but horses can't climb trees. (Yet another useful hint I've given you.)

that means? No one could get in, *but* there was nothing to stop someone getting *out*. Someone, or something . . . or both.

As the group of Pump Street saviours turned the corner of Dank Alley into the main street there was an eye watching them from the door that had been opened a crack.

'Odd place, Fluffy,' the owner of the eye whispered. 'Not so smart as my Rome, of course. But we are free. Can anyone stop me, Fluffy?'

'Nay,' the horse replied.

At the castle, Lady Frankenstone stood in her spotlight and gave her speech. 'People of Wildpool. Tonight you have faced death; you have faced danger; you have faced the most brutal monster the world has ever seen.'

Igon stood beside her. The monster was sitting on the grass below the castle, trapped in his net with each corner held down by the heaviest people in the town. The monster looked defeated.

PC Elloe, Molly and the Crudges slipped in at the back of the crowd.

Igon spoke in the spotlight. 'You faced the dangers bravely. Did you ever give up?'

'No!' the crowd roared back.

'Did you ever despair?'

'No-o-o.'

'Were you ever afraid?'

'Nnnnn ... well ... yes, actually.'

'Your mayor, Lady Greystone, will lock the monster away so children can play on the streets of Wildpool and parents need not worry,' Igon went on.

But her ladyship cut in, 'Until the next show, of course. Come and see it again, if you like, but make sure you tell all your friends. People will flock from every corner of the earth to enjoy what you have enjoyed tonight. Wildpool will be rich with tourists. Your shops will be full of customers; your restaurants will have queues of hungry visitors. All I need to do is knock down Pump Street. What do I have to do?'

'Knock down Pump Street!' the crowd yelled.

Minnie's voice crying, 'Oh, no,' was lost.

But then a squeaky-squawky little voice with a microphone also cried out, 'Oh, no!'

Araminta jumped onto the cab of the wrecking-ball crane and pointed. 'Look at the monster!'

And soon a thousand people were screaming.

The monster can destroy Wildpool and everyone in it?

The monster had gripped the ropes that made up the net and begun to tear at them. The rope was strong. The cords that fastened the ropes were not. First the creature made a hole large enough to push an arm through. It stretched the hole till it had two arms and then its head through.

The crowd began to back away slowly at first, and then fled towards the gate in the wall. The gate had been narrowed so the visitors could only get in two at a time and Brian could take their money.

Now there were a thousand people aiming to get out, not two at a time but a thousand at a time.

The monster's head and shoulders were out of the net now. James King started up the motor of the crane and put it into gear. Araminta was shouting instructions to him as Lady Frankenstone and Igon stood helpless on the top of the walls, looking down.

They saw the skinny figure of Boy race across the parkland towards a shadowed area of the wall. There was a large double gate there where cranes and lorries could enter or leave by a side road. He pulled at the bolts and with a huge effort pulled the massive oak gates open. Boy raced back to the crowd and pointed them towards the new way out. They were now frozen in fear watching the monster's struggles.

'Destroy it with your smartphone app, your ladyship,' Igon moaned.

'I can't. That only works with the infinit-G memory card . . . and Dr Wiggott stole that.'

'That means the monster can destroy Wildpool and everyone in it?' Igon gasped as the heaving mass of panicking people jostled at the gate.

The crane engine roared and the driver began to swing the great iron ball as it rumbled towards the monster. The net was down to its waist now and it was standing up, trying to wrestle its legs free.

The people who'd been fleeing stopped to watch. The screams turned to 'Ooooh's as the last piece of net dropped away and the monster stepped out. It raised its hands in the air and roared.

At that moment the iron ball swung from out of the evening sky. James King was an expert and the ball struck the monster on the side of the head. The head flew off and bounced against the castle wall[60].

The crowd went silent as the monster fell to its knees and began to grope over the grass. At last it found its head and placed it firmly on its neck.

---

60 And your head would do the same if it were hit by a wrecking ball. There is a game, played with a football, called 'Head Tennis'. Do *not* try this with a wrecking ball. You will lose the game. Every time.

'I didn't know it could do that,' Minnie Cooper said.

'It's made of gloop,' Edna explained. 'Every grain of gloop remembers its place in the character. It just re-forms itself.'

'How do you know that, Edna?' Minnie asked.

'Billy works for Dr Wiggott and he tells me these things,' she muttered.

'But that's awful,' Marjorie Doors said. 'It means the monster can never be destroyed.'

'It can be switched off from the smartphone of the person who built it: Lady Frankenstone,' Edna explained.

'So why doesn't she?' Minnie asked.

'Because Boy stole the infinit-G microchip,' Edna moaned. 'We'd have to give the chip back to Lady Frankenstone to stop the monster ... and then she'd make lots of characters for Frankenstone Castle and ruin Dr Wiggott.'

'Is there no answer?' Minnie asked.

The monster had risen to its feet. It tried to take a step and fell over like an old factory chimney brought down by dynamite. And, like a factory chimney, the fall shook the earth.

'What happened?' Igon asked Lady Frankenstone from their perch on the walls of the castle.

'It's confused,' she snapped. 'It put its head on back to front.'

As they watched, the monster stood up, grabbed its ears and twisted the head till it was facing forward. It took a shuffling step forward and nodded, satisfied. It began to walk towards the crowd.

The monster that couldn't be stopped. Except...

This is even better than the monster hunt

The walls of Dank Alley were made of soft and rotten wood. Sounds sank into the damp and were lost. There were not many people left in Wildpool ... they were all at Frankenstone Castle to watch the monster show. But if there had been a stray dog with sharp ears, it would have heard some dull sounds coming from Dank Alley and asked, 'What was that[61]?'

Clop.

'What was that?'

It was the hoof-beat of a horse on cobblestones.

61 What do you mean, 'Dogs don't talk'? Just because you've never heard one doesn't mean talking dogs don't exist. I've never seen the pyramids of Egypt, but that doesn't mean they don't exist. Glad we sorted that.

Click-click-click.

'What was that?'

It was the roll of a chariot wheel over the cobbled alley.

'Hi-ho, Fluffy, away!'

'What was that?'

It was the Emperor Nero giving orders to his horse.

'Uh? That is *crazy*. You don't expect any dog like me to believe that, do you? I'm off to find a nicely scented lamppost.'

Crazy or not, it was true. Nero had followed Molly and PC Elloe out of the Waxworld of ancient Rome, driven down the Waxworld railway and escaped through the door into Dank Alley. Now he was looking for an adventure.

He turned into Wildpool High Street. All he could see was a talking dog sniffing at a lamppost.

But on the hill above the grubby town there were lights flashing and screams as loud as any in the Colosseum. 'That looks like fun,' the emperor chuckled. He turned the horse's head that way and trotted down the empty road. They twisted through the small but neat cottages of Pump Street and into a short stretch of open country. Ahead of Nero stood the castle walls where the gasps and screams were coming from.

The gate into the castle was narrow but a few families had squeezed out. 'Good evening,' Nero called cheerfully. 'Nice evening for a chariot race.'

The nearest family stood open-mouthed. Finally, the mother found her voice. 'Now I've seen everything,' she said. Of course, she hadn't seen everything – no one has – but it's the sort of thing people say when they can't think of anything else to say.

'How does the lord of this castle get his chariot through this gate?' Nero asked.

The youngest child in the family – known by his sisters as Little Clever Clogs – said, 'I believe there is a large gate around the corner ... but it's not a lord, it's a lady. Lady Frankenstone.'

'Strange people,' Nero sighed. He tugged on the reins and trotted along the road to the other gate that Boy had just opened.

Fluffy halted at the gate as Nero looked

inside. Red floodlights made the parkland look eerie and evil. Nero spotted the monster wobbling its way towards the crowds of cowering visitors. 'Wonderful,' he sighed. 'A creature from the underworld. Just the sort of thing Nero the Hero should be destroying. Let's go, horse,' and he slapped the reins. The horse didn't move. 'Nnnng,' Nero growled. 'Hi-ho, Fluffy, away!'

And the horse broke into a canter and raced across the grass towards the monster. The monster heard the pounding hooves and turned to meet the emperor. Nero raised his short sword above his head. The monster raised its arm to grab the man. Nero chopped the arm off.

The crowd gasped.

The monster used its other arm to pick up the one on the ground and push it back in place.

Nero used all his racing skills to skid the chariot round before Fluffy could run into the crowd. Then he launched another attack. He cut to the legs, to the arms, to the head and thrust into the chest. Each time, the monster healed itself ... though it did look a bit annoyed.

The families who'd been trying to run away

returned to see the sport. It was like a gladiators' duel in the Colosseum but without the blood. It was gloop against gloop.

'This is even better than the monster hunt,' Molly said.

'This is grievous bodily harm and it's against the law,' PC Elloe told her.

'Are you going to try to stop them?' Molly asked.

PC L.O. Elloe thought for two milliseconds then replied, 'No.'

'Somebody has to,' Molly said.

And somebody was about to. . .

I'll be revenged on the whole pack of you!

The eyes of Emperor Nero shone star-bright. 'A monster from the myths of Rome,' he cried. 'And I shall defeat it with cleverness.'

He turned Fluffy towards the river that ran fast from Frankenstone Forest and carefully drove the horse in until the water covered the wheels of the chariot. He turned to face the baffled monster. 'Come and get me, you ugly creature from Hell.'

'Uh?' the monster grunted. It began to march towards the river. The Wildpool people began to follow to see what would happen next.

Nero called across the water. 'Come on and fight, you cowardly little man!'

The monster's face was usually blank but now it managed a frown. It bared its teeth and walked faster. It slithered through the mud at the edge of the river.

'Go, Nero, go!' Molly shouted.

From the top of the castle Lady Frankenstone screeched, 'Destroy him, monster!'

The crowd began to join in with chants. 'Go, go, go Ne-ro,' from some, while others shouted, 'Get him, monster, crush and smash! Let's all see the monster mash!'

The monster waded into the water, its arms stretched in front of it. Nero waited till it was close enough, then chopped hard and fast. The hands fell into the water. But the water was fast-flowing and they were washed away before they could join back. As the monster stumbled forward, Nero switched his sword at the creature's neck, and its head flew into the river too. It was washed away. The body sank and Nero raised his sword in triumph.

Some of the crowd cheered him. Others sighed and grumbled, 'I rather liked the monster.'

But the greatest grumbler was Lady Frankenstone. She raged at Igon, 'We had a fortune on our hands. The greatest show Wildpool has ever seen. Destroyed in front of our eyes.'

'Where did that Roman come from?' Igon asked.

'Obvious, silly man. It's one of Dr Wiggott's creations. He has ruined me. And I will take my revenge.'

'How?'

'Tonight, at midnight, when all of Wildpool sleeps, I shall send the wrecking ball to flatten Wiggott's Wonderful Waxworld ... and it can demolish Pump Street as it passes through. I'll be revenged on the whole pack of you[62]!' She turned to Igon. 'Go and see what monster bits you can find in the river. We may be able to put something back together for another show.'

'I'll get my feet wet,' he cried.

'You have more to worry about than wet feet,' Lady Frankenstone snapped. 'That Roman on the chariot will probably get you first.'

---

62 Lady Frankenstone said this ... but she didn't say it. A character said it in a play by William Shakespeare. Lady Frankenstone had learned it at school and always wanted to say it. Always. Now, in her hour of misery, she was happy.

'Great,' Igon said, and went to climb down the steps from the top of the keep.

The mayor wasn't the only one to think Nero was a danger. He walked the horse out of the water and the crowd grew uneasy. They began to hurry towards the gateways to get home and tucked up in bed. But Nero's eyes were fixed on one person. Molly.

She stood firm, but even in the red glow of the floodlights she looked pale.

'The girl from my Colosseum. The one who fired the poison darts at me.' He stopped the chariot alongside her.

'It was a Taser, actually.'

'It was cheating,' Nero said, and his voice was suddenly soft as the grass. He looked at PC Elloe. 'And you gave her the weapon.' He slowly raised the sword that was still dripping with gloop from the monster's ruined body. 'I'll be revenged on the whole pack of you,' he said. (When Dr Wiggott programmed Nero, a little Shakespeare had slipped in.) 'Prepare to die.'

Molly and PC Elloe prepared by closing

their eyes. The Taser had no charge. The truncheon was left on the floor of the Colosseum. Nothing could save them. Except...

Edna destroyed
the thing

Have you ever seen a jelly on a plate? Someone shakes the table and it shivers and shimmers, quivers and quakes, trembles and totters[63].

That was how Nero looked. The colour faded from him and his chariot and Fluffy till they were clear as water ... or clear as gloop ... which is what they were. In a few moments the gloop collapsed into a puddle on the grass.

Molly opened one eye to see what had happened. PC Elloe opened one eye. They opened four eyes between them.

---

63 If you *haven't* seen a jelly on a plate, then you have led a very sad life. What is a party without a jelly? It is like a dog without a tail.

Boy spoke for them all. 'How did that happen?'

'I don't know,' Molly whispered, and her knees shook like gloop.

Minnie's sharp eyes had seen what happened. 'Edna Crudge took out her smartphone,' she told Molly. 'Edna opened an app and pressed a button. Edna destroyed the thing.'

'How did you do that, Edna?' Marjorie Doors asked. 'I thought Dr Wiggott was the only one with a controller.'

'My Billy gave it to me, in case there was a problem,' she answered, but her voice was as weak as Molly's knees, which (you will remember) were as weak as watery gloop.

'Nero was a nasty character anyway,' Marjorie Doors said with a sniff. 'We're better off without him roaming round Wildpool. He's nearly as nasty as that Lady Frankenstone,' she added. Their eyes turned to the castle where the mayor looked down on them with eyes as fierce and angry as Taser darts.

The rest of the visitors had gone home happy and the sound-and-light team were packing away their gear. The woman with dark curling hair, known to Lady Frankenstone as 'Call-me-Charlie' was moving her workers out quickly.

The Ladies Who Crunch led the way back down the road to Wildpool. 'I think the mayor's eyes said Revenge,' Marjorie said. 'Pump Street could be flattened tonight.'

'I know,' Minnie said as they reached her front door. 'Come in for a cup of tea and I'll tell you the clever plan we have concocted to put a stop to that.'

She lit a fire in her hearth to keep away the chill of the night air, which was always damp in Wildpool. They crowded into the little cottage and drank tea around Minnie's table while they listened to the plan.

'I'm a policeman,' PC L.O. Elloe said. 'I can't be part of that.'

'I know, young man. That's why I have a special job for you. I want you to go on duty. Patrol near the castle. As soon as you hear the crane engine start up, I want you to phone Edna here. Give him your number, Edna.'

Marjorie Doors smirked. 'Getting bossy in your old age, Minnie?'

'I'll be as bossy as it takes to save Pump Street. Some of us have lived here all our lives and we're not letting that wicked woman drive us out,' the little grey-haired lady said.

PC Elloe left to walk up to the castle. It was midnight when Edna's phone rang. She nodded, cut the call and looked around the room. 'It's starting.' She turned to Boy. 'Off you go. You know what to do[64].'

64 But would *you* know what to do? Maybe not, because you don't have the Ladies Who Crunch to help – and remember, they make the best plans in the world.

Bet you can't hit that spot first time

Boy was thief-trained by an expert – Edna Crudge. So, he knew how to move quickly. He was almost invisible in his dark-grey clothes, and silent in his rubber-soled trainers.

The night sky was thick with grey, cotton-wool clouds that blanked out the moonlight. *Perfect for the plan*, Boy thought.

It took him just two minutes to flit past Loaf Tower, dark and quiet as the glass that it was made from. Half a minute later he was at the doors to the Wildpool Power Station. He let himself in with the key he'd stolen from the man with a head like hairy cabbage.

Moments later he stood in front of the control panel and grinned at the large red master-switch. He snapped it to the 'off' position and everything in Wildpool turned dark as a mole's belly.

He used the light from his phone to find his way back to the door. He locked it and snapped off the key in the lock. The man with the head of a hairy cabbage wouldn't be able to use his spare key to get in. A locksmith could open it in ten minutes. But where would you find a locksmith at midnight[65]?

Using the light from his phone, Boy sped back up to Pump Street and on towards the castle. He'd been so fast, the Ladies Who Crunch had only just reached the door in the wall of the Frankenstone estate.

'Go and take a nap, Constable Elloe,' Edna said quietly. 'You don't need to see what happens next. Just wait outside the walls on that bench over there till we call you inside.' He nodded and in his dark navy uniform was soon lost in the night.

---

65 No, please don't answer that. It's not a serious question. If you know of any midnight locksmiths, I don't want you writing to tell me. Very kind of you to offer, but no thanks.

James King had switched on the engine of the crane and it rumbled away. Boy put on the skull-cap and eyepatch that Marjorie Doors had knitted for him and ran across to the crane cab as Molly and the Ladies Who Crunch went to their positions. Boy called up to the cab, 'Hello, James?'

'Who's there?'

Boy flashed his phone-torch on himself very quickly, then towards James King, so the driver was a little blinded. 'It's me, Igon. We've killed the electrics in Wildpool till dawn, so you can do this in secret.'

'How do I find my way to the houses her ladyship wants knocked down?' James King asked.

'We've thought of that. We have a team of workers from Loaf Tower with torches. They'll point their beams to the spots on the walls that we want you to hit.'

'But how do I get to Pump Street without putting my headlights on?'

'Easy. Just follow my torch,' Boy said and turned the torch onto the windscreen of the crane cab, so James King was still a little dazzled. Boy led the way around the parkland surrounding the castle keep for ten minutes – the time it would take the crane to reach Pump Street. Then he called up to the driver, 'See the spot where the torch is shining?' He pointed to where Molly held the beam of her torch against a wall. 'Bet you can't hit that spot first time,' Boy shouted.

'Bet I can,' the driver laughed. He swung the jib of the crane a few times to get up some force then smashed it into Molly's light spot. The spot that – as you've guessed – was shining on the wall of Frankenstone Castle.

Somewhere deep inside the castle, Lady Frankenstone was in her bed, reading by candlelight, when the room shuddered and shook. She looked out of the window to see what had happened but all she could see was the thin beam of a phone-torch.

In the kitchens downstairs, pans were sent flying off their hooks on the wall and Igon raced for the door. But the wrecking ball had smashed the frame and he couldn't get out. He sat in the tangle of pans and stone-dust and waited for the next blow that could bring down the ceiling.

But that wasn't part of Minnie Cooper's plan. Her friends led the crane around the park and punched holes in the outside walls.

Deep into the night Minnie had the pleasure of doing the final act – she led the crane into the river by Frankenstone Forest. The water rushed and gushed over the engine. It coughed, it hissed, it sizzled and spluttered, then died.

PC Elloe was called from his seat outside and marched in with his handcuffs to arrest James King, who had waded ashore. 'What's the charge?' he wailed.

'Criminal damage,' PC Elloe replied. 'You have half demolished Frankenstone Castle. It's a night in the cells for you, sir.'

'Oh dear,' Minnie muttered as the team gathered at the gates and walked wearily down the hill and back to their beds. 'I feel almost sorry for Lady Frankenstone.'

Oddly the others nodded and said, 'Me too.'

They went home and arranged to meet in Wiggott's Wonderful Waxworld the next morning – *late* the next morning, after a long sleep.

He'll not be flattening any cottages for a long time

Wildpool woke to the quiet smell of dust. A thin cloud of powdered stone drifted down from Frankenstone Castle and settled on the clothes on Wildpool washing-lines.

Lady Frankenstone walked out of the castle door and stood beside Igon, looking around at the damage. 'Wonderful,' the mayor said with a sigh.

'Not really,' Igon moaned. 'It'll take years to repair.'

'Why would I want to repair it?' her ladyship asked. 'People love ruined castles more than anything. They look like the scene of a great battle. Of knights in days of old...'

'Nights in days?' Igon asked.

Lady Frankenstone ignored him. 'Picture it: armoured men and women on horseback charging through the broken walls ... the beautiful lady in red at the top of the tower, waiting to be rescued...'

'That'll be you,' the little man muttered.

'It will be even better than the Frankenstone monster story.'

Igon held up a thumb and finger. He ticked them off. 'One, we have no infinit-G chip.'

'I know where to get one,' the woman in red smirked.

'Two, Pump Street is still a problem. Traffic can't get through to the castle.'

'So, we let the tourists walk. They can collect costumes from Loaf Tower when they arrive. There'll be no modern machines at the castle. The tourists will walk through the narrow lanes – lanes like Pump Street – just like people did in the Middle Ages. They'll walk into the past. It will be brilliant, Igon. Brilliant. Just like me.'

The man sighed. 'If you say so.'

She rubbed her hands. 'Let's get started,' she said and marched towards the front gate.

'Where are we going?' Igon asked.

'Where? To Wiggott's Wonderful Waxworld, of course.'

Boy and Molly met at the entrance to Dank Alley.

PC Elloe plodded past. 'There was a lot of trouble up at Frankenstone Castle last night,' he said with a wink at the boy and girl. 'I've arrested a crane driver called James King. He'll not be flattening any cottages for a long time.'

'Thank you, Constable,' Molly said. 'We couldn't have saved Minnie's home without you. You're the best policeman in the whole of Wildpool.'

'No, he's not,' Boy said. Molly blinked. Boy went on, 'He's the best policeman in the whole world.'

PC L.O. Elloe tapped his helmet in a salute and said, 'Mornin' all,' before plodding off down the street.

Molly led the way into Dank Alley that was greasy and dull as ever. Rats scurried away and hid in holes in the wooden walls. They knocked three times on the back door to Wiggott's Wonderful Waxworld[66].

Rap-rap-rap.

Billy Crudge opened the door and let them in to the dim Waxworld. 'Minnie and Marjorie are here already. Edna's too busy,' he explained.

He led the way into the computer room with gloop on the table and the computers humming ... they still didn't know the words. A new model of Nero was slowly taking shape.

Billy cleared his throat and began. 'We're here to decide what to do next. Roman world is working.'

'It was scary.' Molly nodded.

'So what's next?' Minnie asked.

'Good question,' a woman answered from the doorway. The Wiggott's Waxworld team turned and looked at the open door where the newcomer stood.

'What are you doing here?' Molly asked, fiercely.

---

66 No, no, no. Boy and Molly knocked at the door, not the rats. Stop being silly.

The man with an eyepatch scowled. 'That's no way to speak to your mayor,' he said.

'I'm here to help you,' Lady Frankenstone said with a smile.

And this is the new Dr Wiggott speaking

'I have a castle that looks great now, thanks to your little plot,' Lady Frankenstone said.

'The Ladies Who Crunch always have the best plans,' Minnie said proudly.

'As I say, I have the castle, Dr Wiggott has the infinit-G chips ... the ones he stole from Loaf Tower.'

'You're not getting them back,' Billy said sharply.

'I have an idea I want to put to Dr Wiggott,' the mayor said.

'No one gets to see Dr Wiggott,' Marjorie Doors said.

'And I'm sure he wouldn't want to talk to you,' Boy began.

A large screen on the wall flashed into life. A picture appeared of a man with a large moustache, wearing a top hat and a red coat. He looked like the ringmaster in a circus. 'That's the old Dr Wiggott,' Minnie said. 'The one that built this place. He died thirty years ago and then the new Dr Wiggott took over.'

'Correct,' a voice from the screen said. It was a creaking voice of the sort you get when you ask a computer to speak to you. 'And this is the new Dr Wiggott speaking.'

Lady Frankenstone rose to her feet and faced the screen. 'Good morning, Doctor. I don't know why you are disguising your voice – or why no one can get to see you...'

'Because some of the things I have done have been against the law,' the voice said.

'Like stealing infinit-G chips from Loaf Tower?'

'Yes. I have done many shady things to keep this old Waxworld open.'

'Then let me help you,' the woman said.

Minnie and Marjorie, Boy and Molly all started to talk at once. Shocked. 'Shhhh,' Dr Wiggott's voice calmed them. 'Sit down and let us listen.'

'You are a genius,' the woman in red said.

'Thank you – that's true,' the Doctor said[67].

'Your Nero was brilliant last night. Thrilling. But this building is in a terrible state. What you need is a lot of money to smarten it up and build new worlds.'

There was a short silence. 'I do.'

'I have money,' Lady Frankenstone said. 'I could give you enough to make this wreck of a building into Wiggott's Wonderful New Waxworld.'

'Go on,' Dr Wiggott, said and everyone in the Wiggott's Waxworld team strained their ears and popped their eyes that the doctor was even willing to talk about it.

'Let's share the infinit-G chips. . .'

'No,' Boy cried. 'The trouble I went to get them.'

---

67 A top tip for you there. If someone says something nice about you then do two things. Say 'Thank you' . . . and then agree with them.

'Shush, Boy, let's listen,' said Dr Wiggott.

Lady Frankenstone explained. 'I can put on Marvellous Middle Ages shows in the ruins of my castle. The characters are all made of gloop so there is no risk, and no one gets hurt. But it will look fantastic.'

'It's in the open air,' Molly said. 'No one would go there in a Wildpool winter.'

Lady Frankenstone nodded. 'Exactly. So where do visitors go in the cold weather?'

Minnie Cooper clapped her hands. 'They come here, to Wiggott's,' she cried.

'Instead of battling against each other,' Billy Crudge said, 'we join forces?'

Igon managed a smile on his grim face. 'It's a battle that we both end up winning.'

Even Boy was silenced by the sense of this.

'Do we have a deal, Dr Wiggott?' the mayor asked.

'Almost,' the voice said finally. 'Just one thing.'

'What's that?'

'I am getting very old. I'm as old *now* as my father, the first Dr Wiggott, was when he died thirty years ago. I'm too old to start again. I will sign the Waxworld over to some young and fresh people. From now on, Lady Frankenstone, you work with Molly Maltby and Boy, while I retire.'

The mayor nodded. 'They are bright and brave, young and full of energy. I bet they'd be full of new ideas.'

'Well. . . I did think. . .' Molly Maltby began.

'Me too,' Boy cut in.

'It's a deal, then,' Lady Frankenstone said before they could start an argument.

Minnie Cooper picked up her cup of tea and raised it in the air. 'Here's to Wiggott's Wonderful New Waxworld.'

'To Wiggott's Wonderful New Waxworld,' everyone cheered.

The gloop that was the new Nero blinked and sat up. 'But what will Edna Crudge say when she hears the plan?'

Billy Crudge gave a small smile. 'She'll love it,' he said.

'How do you know?' Molly asked.

'I just *know*,' Billy said.

It's not too late to seek a newer world

The new friends left the Waxworld and wandered down Dank Alley sharing ideas, as excited as a rat at an open bin by the back of a burger bar.

Billy Crudge wandered wearily out of his office. He switched off his computer and the bright screen faded. He rubbed his tired eyes.

A few wise words were printed and framed and hung on the wall above his desk. They read:

Working together works
Dr Wilbur Wiggott (1906–1990)

'Good old Wilbur,' Billy chuckled. 'A great inventor ... but not so great as *our* Dr Wiggott.'

Through the dusty windows of the office he could see the wooden trains standing by the side of the track, clicking and cooling. The tiny lights in the roof of Wiggott's Wonderful Waxworld sparkled like the stars they were supposed to be.

'Stars belong in the sky,' the caretaker said. 'A place for everything, everything in its place. A bit like Minnie Cooper and that house of hers.'

There was a soft hiss and a faint crackle as a speaker on the wall came alive. 'Get along to my office now, Billy Crudge,' a voice snapped.

'Yes, Dr Wiggott,' the man sighed.

He walked through a door at the back of his office and down a dim corridor that led to the very heart of the Waxworlds. From the twenty doors, he chose one. He tapped with his gnarled old knuckle. 'Come in,' the voice said.

He opened the door, looked in at the lamp-lit desk and the large and shapeless figure that sat behind it. 'Good evening, Dr Wiggott. It's been a good day. Like your dad always said, working together works.'

'Yes, Billy, Wildpool is a better place because of all our work today,' Dr Wiggott agreed.

'But?' Billy said quietly. 'I feel you are thinking about saying a "but".'

'But we are getting old. We can't go on for ever. Still, I'll miss this place.'

Billy nodded. 'But Wildpool is in safe hands so long as young people like Boy and Molly are around ... and even PC Elloe.'

'True,' Dr Wiggott agreed.

'So, we can retire? Leave the Waxworld in their safe hands and put our feet up for the last of our days?'

There was a long, deep sigh. 'No. We're old ... but there's still a place for us here. I know, I *told* them I was planning to retire. But I hate that word.'

'Me too.' Billy nodded.

'When I went to school we learned a poem by a bloke called Tennyson,' Dr Wiggott went on and the voice was like someone speaking in a dream. 'Tennyson told a story of some adventurers who wanted one last great adventure. I remember the words to this day, "Come, my friends, 'tis not too late to seek a newer world."'

'Not too late?' Billy echoed. 'So, Dr Wiggott is off to seek a newer world?'

'Not Dr Wiggott. *This* Dr Wiggott is giving up the Waxworld job and moving on. Take the keys to the Waxworld and give them to Molly. She can be the next Dr Wiggott, just like I was when my old dad packed things in.'

Billy Crudge nodded and jangled the keys in his ancient hand. 'Does that mean I don't have to call you Dr Wiggott any more?'

'That's right, Billy,' Dr Wiggott said. 'Call me by my proper name. Edna. My married name, Edna Crudge.'

Billy grinned. 'Come, my Edna. It's not too late to seek a newer world,' he said. He took her hand. 'And we mustn't forget to turn the lights off on the way out.'

The stars in Wiggott's Wonderful Waxworld flickered and died. The Waxworlds and the trains stood silent apart from the soft fall of dust and the whirring of spinning spiders.

Who knew when Wiggott's Wonderful Waxworld would wake again to laughter and chills and thrills and voices shrill?

But it would.

Who knew where Edna and Billy would find their newer world?

But they would.

They left the old Waxworld arm in arm.

More from Terry Deary

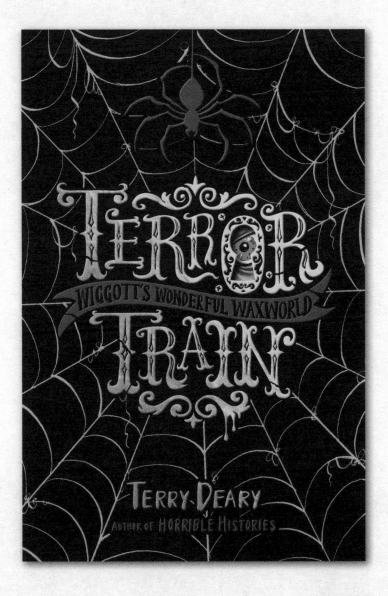

TERROR

WIGGOTT'S WONDERFUL WAXWORLD

TRAIN

TERRY DEARY

AUTHOR OF HORRIBLE HISTORIES

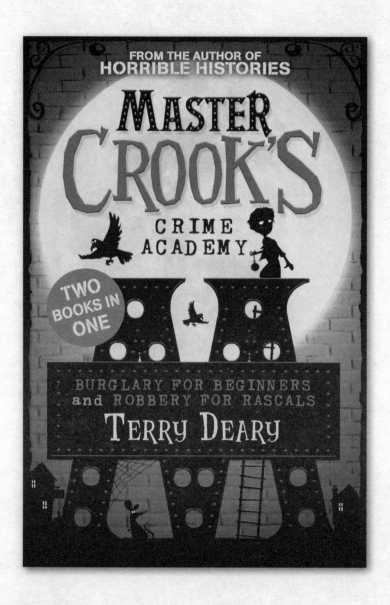

FROM THE AUTHOR OF
HORRIBLE HISTORIES

MASTER CROOK'S

CRIME ACADEMY

TWO
BOOKS IN
ONE

BURGLARY FOR BEGINNERS
and ROBBERY FOR RASCALS

TERRY DEARY

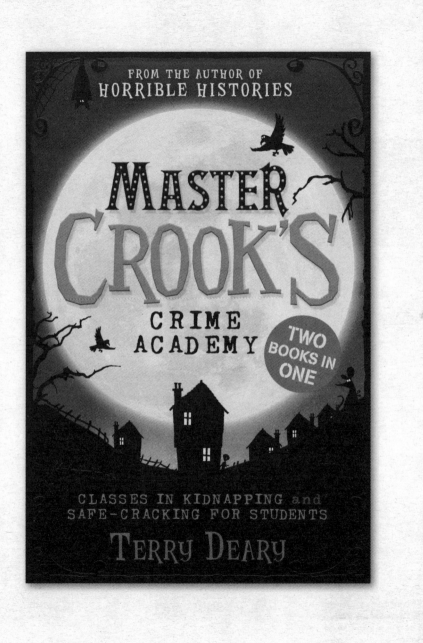

FROM THE AUTHOR OF
HORRIBLE HISTORIES

MASTER CROOK'S

CRIME
ACADEMY

TWO BOOKS IN ONE

CLASSES IN KIDNAPPING and
SAFE-CRACKING FOR STUDENTS

TERRY DEARY